Hers to Take

Bears of Grizzly Ridge

Elena Aitken

Hers to Take: Bears of Grizzly Ridge, 4

Ink Blot Communications
ISBN: 978-1-927968-64-2

Also by Elena

Grizzly Ridge
His to Protect
His to Seduce
His to Claim
Hers to Take

The Springs
Summer of Change
Falling Into Forever
Winter's Burn
Midnight Springs
Second Glances
She's Making A List

Stone Summit Series
Summit of Desire
Summit of Seduction
Summit of Passion

CHAPTER ONE

"I really am sorry, ma'am. But as I've tried to explain, we just don't have any riverfront sites available for a unit your size." Kira Jackson spoke as sweetly as she could. Not that it mattered, because the woman who'd been demanding Kira upgrade her family's campsite to one of the premium spots still didn't look as though she was prepared to take no for an answer.

The truth was, even if Kira did have a campsite available in May—the start of the summer season—that would fit the nasty woman's monstrosity of an apartment on wheels, she likely still wouldn't have given it to her. Not that she was vindictive; it was just that reserving the prime spots for nice families who were on their once-in-a-lifetime family vacations to Yellowstone National Park was definitely more rewarding than giving them out to people like the woman in front of her, who'd been spewing all kinds of venom from the moment she'd walked up to Kira's window.

"I demand to speak to your manager." The woman slammed her fist on the counter.

With her practiced smile still on her face, Kira took a step back and turned away. *She could speak to a manager all right.* Too bad Kira *was* the manager. Not that she was about to volunteer that information. Because Kira seriously doubted it would make any difference to the woman.

"Sasha, there's a woman who would like to speak to you." Kira spoke through clenched teeth to her co-worker, who'd just returned from a break. Sasha instantly identified the problem. Sadly, it was a little too common for either of their liking.

"I'll handle this." Sasha patted Kira on the shoulder as she walked by. "Why don't you go check the wood supply?"

Kira knew enough to take the out when it was offered. With a sigh of relief, she left Sasha and the unreasonable woman behind and headed outside where they kept the overpriced boxes of wood they sold to the tourists who, despite the cramped campgrounds, wanted to feel as if they were really camping in Yellowstone.

Not that it was a bad place. Not at all. And besides the occasional bad guest, for the most part Kira enjoyed her job in Yellowstone. It was the perfect place for a bear shifter to hang out. Well, maybe not the *perfect* place. That would be back home in Jackson Valley with her family. But that was no longer an option.

She sighed and straightened her shoulders. There was no point dwelling on the fact that she likely wasn't welcome at home anymore. Especially considering it was her own fault. *No. Yellowstone was her home now.* And as far as places she could have picked to start over, it was pretty good.

Her job allowed her to work in the woods, where she could sneak off to let her bear run free when she needed to, which was less and less these days. She was relatively left alone to manage the Riverside campground on her own. As long as she was doing her job well, and running things efficiently, her bosses didn't seem to care what she did. The people she worked with were nice enough, which was a good thing because they lived together in a small grouping of even smaller cabins behind the registration office.

She inhaled deeply and let out the breath slowly before she walked toward the wood pile. Selling the boxes for twenty dollars each didn't deter the tourists from buying them up, and the office was getting low. With the holiday weekend around the corner, they would definitely need to stock up. Which meant Kira needed to split the logs and fill the boxes.

Sasha thought Kira was crazy for always volunteering for the job, but ever since she was a little girl, Kira had always loved splitting wood. Her two oldest brothers, Axel and Luke, always tried to tell her she was too little, and girls shouldn't try to do a boy's job. A theory their grandfather subscribed to as well. It was Kade, her twin brother, who'd let her try his ax for the first time and taught her how to hold it. They'd always had a special relationship. A twin bond.

They used to be inseparable.

Used to be.

Kira shook it off and forced herself to focus on the present. It was getting harder and harder to avoid thinking of her brothers, especially Kade, but she'd made her choice and she'd live with it. No matter what.

She picked up the ax, set up the first log and hefted the ax over her head before she swung her arms down. Hard.

The log split easily. She picked up the smaller piece and repeated the action again and again, until finally her arms began to strain from the effort. She could have kept going, but Sasha's voice stopped her.

"You're a machine."

Kira turned to see her friend leaning against the wall, watching with wide eyes. She made a show of wiping her brow, despite the fact that she'd barely worked up a sweat.

"You've barely been out here twenty minutes." Sasha walked toward her. "How did you do that so fast?"

Kira shrugged. "Once I get going, I just get into a groove or something. Besides, we needed wood, so…"

"Still." Sasha shook her head in disbelief. "You must have had some aggression to work out after Mrs. McCarthy."

"Was that her name?" Kira propped the ax up against the chopping block. "She was something else. How did you manage to make her happy?"

Sasha laughed. "I told her a riverfront spot had just opened up that you didn't know about."

Kira raised her eyebrows and listened with interest.

"I gave her site 58."

"Site 58? The one behind the old outhouses?"

Sasha nodded and Kira couldn't help but laugh. "But did you see the size of their trailer? It would only—"

"Just fit?" Sasha smiled an evil grin. "Exactly. They'd be able to back in, nice and tight to the toilets. I'd be surprised if they could see the lake at all once they get in there."

"You're evil."

"I think you mean evil genius."

"Of course that's what I meant." Kira laughed. "Thanks for taking care of that for me."

"That's what I'm here for. Besides, I was kind of hoping you'd be so thankful that you'd go out and meet the maintenance guy for me in the shower house."

Inwardly, Kira groaned. Dealing with Cranky Carl, as he was referred to by the campsite staff, was typically a job they drew straws for and it was Sasha's turn. The old guy was fairly handy, but he far preferred to complain about it first. For at least an hour.

"You owe me," Sasha reminded her.

"Okay." She pulled the elastic out of her thick black hair

and refastened it into a ponytail. She hoped she didn't have too many wood chips stuck in her hair. "But you're boxing the wood."

"Deal." Sasha tossed her the keys to the quad they used to get around the campground and disappeared back inside. Likely before Kira could change her mind.

She'd done a lot worse, and Cranky Carl wasn't nearly as bad as her grandfather used to get when he got mad at her brothers when they were cubs. The three of them always could fire up the old man, almost as if they made a sport of it. Come to think of it, they probably did. Not that they would have told Kira. She had definitely been her grandfather's little princess. She could do no wrong.

Except once.

Dammit. Why were thoughts of home intruding on her life today? It had been almost two years since she'd left. Two years since her brothers had come looking for her. And two years since she'd turned her back and sent them away. And all for a mate.

No!

For a man she *thought* had been her fated mate. She'd been wrong. And now there was no going back. She'd made her choice, and she'd just have to live with it. Just as she'd turned her back on her twin brother, he'd very clearly done the same to her. For months, she'd tried to reach out to him. The connection they shared was heightened because of their twin bond. When they were in bear form, they should be able to sense each other. Especially if the other was in some sort of pain or distress. And she had been. Every day since she'd left home, Kira felt the pain of the loss deep in her gut.

But Kade had never reached out to her. Every chance she got, Kira would shift into her bear and run through the forest, calling out for her brother. Even with the distance between them, there should have been something. Some connection to let her know she wasn't alone.

But there'd been nothing. And she hadn't tried in months. *What was the point?*

She'd accepted her new life. Mostly. But days like today when the memories flooded back were hard.

Kira fired up the ATV and put it in gear, headed to the shower house where two of the stalls had been backing up. Dealing with Cranky Carl would be a good distraction; at least she wouldn't have to think about anything else but clogged drains and broken showers.

There were about a thousand other things Nash North would have rather been doing than sticking his hand down the clogged-up, nasty ass drain of a shower stall in a public campground. When he took the job as the resident handyman for the summer, he hadn't given the job description much thought. Or any thought, really. All Nash cared about was a place to stay and a few dollars in his pocket while he figured out his next move.

Now that he was elbow deep in other people's hair and some sort of sludge he probably didn't even want to identify, Nash was definitely second-guessing taking the job without paying any attention to what he'd be doing.

He wiggled his fingers around the clog and tried not to think about what he might actually be touching when his sharp senses tuned into the footsteps of someone approaching.

A female.

He didn't look up, but Nash wasn't surprised when a moment later a sexy, smooth voice, with just a hint of an edge, asked, "What exactly are you doing?"

Without removing his hand from the drain, he looked up into the dark eyes of a woman every bit as sexy as her voice.

More so. She was tall, although not likely as tall as he was, with strong, luscious curves beneath her parks uniform. The animal inside him responded immediately to the sight of her long, thick ponytail hanging down her back, her arms crossed over her ample chest, and the fire in her eyes as she stared down at him.

Maybe the job wouldn't be so bad after all.

"I'm fixing your drain, darlin'."

She narrowed her eyes. "I'm not your darlin'. And you're not Cranky Carl."

"No." Nash latched on to a wad of hair and sludge in the drain and yanked. "I'm definitely not Carl." He grinned. "And I'm not cranky. But I just fixed your drain." He wiped his hand on a rag and stood.

Damn. The woman was even more impressive when she was directly in front of him. And she was definitely not human. He held out his now clean hand. "Nash North."

Her dark eyes narrowed and she took a moment to look him over. She could have taken all day as far as Nash was concerned. Her gaze felt good. Damn good. Because if she liked what she saw even half as much as he liked the sight of her, it was going to be an interesting summer indeed. Finally, she took his hand.

"Kira Jackson." Her grip was strong, her skin soft, her touch electric. "Where's Carl?"

"Cranky Carl?" He raised an eyebrow.

"I shouldn't have said that." Kira slipped her hand from his and Nash had to fight the instinct to grab it back. "It's just that Carl can be a little..."

"Cranky?"

She tipped her head and for a moment she looked as though she might disagree, but finally she nodded. "Yes. He can be a little cranky from time to time."

"Well then, I guess it's an appropriate nickname," Nash said. "I can't tell you where he is, but I was told that I was hired on because the man before me retired. So perhaps he's a little less cranky now?"

"One can only hope." Kira smiled reluctantly. "At least for his wife's sake."

"Oh, I can't imagine Carl is married."

"Are you?" The question was out of his mouth so fast, and so smoothly, it clearly took her a second to process it. Nash could see when she did.

Kira shook her head, looked away and took a step to the side. "I don't think so."

"You don't think you're married?"

"Oh, I *know* I'm not married." Kira spun around, her eyes blazing, making them look even darker than before. "Not that it's any of your business."

He knew he was being forward and presumptuous, but that had never stopped him before. "Mated then?" Nash could have sworn he heard a growl come from deep within her. And in that moment, he knew. *A bear. Damn.* He should have seen it right away, but there was something about her. Her animal was muted somehow.

"How the...what...you..."

"Wolf."

"Wolf?" She almost spat out the word. Nash took a step back and crossed his arms over his chest.

"You don't have to sound so damned disgusted about it."

"No." Kira shook her head apologetically and closed her eyes for a moment. "That's not what I...sorry...I didn't realize."

And that's what was wrong. She *hadn't* realized he was a shifter. It was unusual for a shifter not to recognize another. Even a different species. But then again, he hadn't recognized

Elena Aitken

her as a bear. Not right away, anyway.

"Is that going to be a problem?" Nash tilted his head and watched her for a moment while she clearly had an internal battle he didn't understand. "Because, judging by the look on your face…it might be a problem."

"No." Kira shook her head quickly and bit her bottom lip, an action that sent a flash of desire right to his core. *Damn. The woman was sexy and had no idea.* "It's fine. I was just taken off guard is all."

"Were you?" He took a step toward her. As he expected, she didn't back away. Bears never did. Kira straightened and her deep, dark eyes stared directly into his.

"I was preoccupied was all. I wasn't expecting to walk in here and find a *wolf.*" It wasn't his imagination; there was definitely disdain laced through her voice. "I was coming to deal with a clogged shower and Cranky Carl. I was not expecting *you.*"

Nash took another half step toward her and rubbed the stubble on his chin as he challenged her with, "Well, you got me, babe."

"I'm not your babe."

"Not yet."

"No." She shook her head and stepped toward him, straightening up to her full height. *Bear or not, he wanted her. Badly.* "This isn't happening." Nash expected her to step closer, closing the gap. In his experience, bears didn't back down. Especially to wolves. Instead, she turned and walked to the door before she looked back at him. "If you plan on keeping your job, this isn't going to happen." Kira gestured between them. "I don't know if you were told, but I'm the manager of this campground and won't tolerate—"

"Me?"

"No." She glared at him. "I won't tolerate

9

your…your…this."

She bit her lip again and Nash tried not to react. She'd calm down, but she was right. If he wanted to keep his job—and he did—he couldn't afford to piss her off. Even if it was fun to watch her get riled up. And it was. If there was one thing Nash enjoyed, it was to have fun with a sexy woman. "I'm sorry." But he also knew when to swallow it and play the game and in this instance, he was all about the game. Especially if it meant keeping his job. "I came here to clean up a clogged shower." He gave her his most genuine smile. "I definitely wasn't expecting to meet a beautiful bear while I had my hand down the drain."

His words didn't make everything better, but Kira's shoulders lost some of the tension and she no longer looked as if she was going to go for his jugular.

"At any rate," he said, pouring on the charm, "I didn't mean to come on so strong. Please accept my apologies."

He waited for a moment while she considered it. Nash half expected her to say no and fire him, or at the very least storm out. Bears weren't known for their ability to calm down quickly or, especially when it came to wolves, be reasonable. But Kira was definitely not a usual bear. In fact, she was very different from any other bear he'd ever encountered. And he was intrigued. To say the least.

"Okay," she said after what seemed like a very long time. "I accept your apology." She nodded toward the drain he'd just unclogged. "Thanks for that."

Nash waited until she'd turned her head and taken a few steps toward the door before he let himself smile. *He was really going to like this job.*

"Oh, and before you go." Kira turned around so suddenly, Nash swallowed his smile. "Check the other drains, and I heard there was a toilet that needed snaking. Could you see to that?"

He resisted the urge to salute. "Absolutely."

She gave him a look and for a second, he thought she might say something else. Instead, Kira nodded. "Good."

Nash didn't even try to contain his smile as he watched her juicy curves in her tight khaki pants walking away. *Oh, yes. The summer was definitely turning around for the better.* Was it really only a few weeks ago he'd left his big brother and his pack in search of something....well, just *something?* Things had certainly turned around. Clogged drains and toilets aside, not only did Nash have a job for the summer, he had a place to sleep, and with any luck, before long he'd have a very sexy she-bear to cuddle up with to keep that bed warm.

CHAPTER TWO

"A wolf?"

Kira stalked toward the cabins where the staff lived. She'd driven the ATV back from the shower house faster than she should have. Faster than the vehicle should move, period. But she needed to burn off some steam. What she needed to do was shift and let her bear out. But she wasn't doing that.

Not anymore.

There was no point in shifting.

There hadn't been for a very long time. But she hadn't ever before felt the burn in her veins, the heat that coursed through her, threatening to consume her. Something about Nash had triggered a response in her that heightened the need to shift into her bear, to run, to feel the animal inside her.

It wasn't an option.

"Dammit." She kicked a stone in her path. "A bloody wolf."

"A wolf?"

Kira spun on her heel to see Sasha next to the wood pile. "Did you say there was a wolf? Here? In the campsite?"

"No." She had to think fast. After all, there was a wolf in the campsite, but not one Kira could talk about. "No," she told Sasha. "I was just thinking about something else." "You're sure? You look concerned about something." "I'm fine." Kira forced a smile she didn't feel. "And really, it's nothing. I was just thinking about something I read in the newsletter about the wolves in the park." That wasn't entirely a lie. She had been reading about the Yellowstone-wide wolf reintroduction project and how some packs had thrived while others had failed. Kira couldn't help but wonder which one of those packs Nash had come from. Or whether he was a Yellowstone wolf at all.

Not that she was going to ask.

She was *definitely not* going to ask him.

"Hello. Earth to Kira." Sasha waved a hand in front of her face. "Are you okay? You look like you've seen a ghost."

Not a ghost. A wolf. A tall, sexy...

"I'm fine," Kira said. "I was just thinking about—"

"The shower room?" Sasha laughed. "What exactly went on over there?" Before Kira could come up with a decent excuse, Sasha's pretty face changed and her mouth fell into an O. "You met the new handyman, right?"

"What?"

"The new handyman. You met him, didn't you?"

"You knew Cranky Carl was gone?"

"Well, I didn't know *know*. But I'd heard." She winked. "And I saw a super hottie in a truck earlier, was that him? Judging by the look on your face, it was. It totally should have been me who went to check on the shower house. Damn."

Irritation rose in Kira. She didn't want there to be any look at all about her when it came to Nash. "What look on my face?"

Sasha did a little wiggly dance and her black curls bounced around her head. *"That* look!"

Kira stuck her hands on her hips and stared at her friend until she stopped dancing.

"Oh come on." Sasha laughed. "Judging by your face, I'd say you've just seen the sexiest man to ever set foot into this campsite. Am I wrong?"

She wasn't wrong. "I guess Nash is—"

"Nash?" Sasha put her hand to her chest and swooned. "That's his name? Oh my God. Of course that's his name. He would have to have a totally hot name. It suits him, don't you think?"

Kira shook her head. She was not going to have this conversation. She didn't even want to think about him and his steel-gray eyes that seemed to see right through her and sense her need. Or the way his lean muscles filled out his parks uniform, or— "I guess he's attractive, if you like that type."

Sasha snorted a laugh. "That type? Of course I like that type. Who *doesn't* like that type? Damn, girl. I only saw him from a distance, but that is definitely a type I'd like to see close up. Really close up, if you know what I mean?"

Kira knew exactly what her friend meant, and it wasn't going to happen. If Sasha knew Nash was really a wolf shifter, she would freak out. *Probably.* The alternative was that her friend would be even more attracted to Nash and the last thing Kira needed to deal with that summer was a relationship between a wolf and a human. Particularly when that human was her friend and wolves were... well, wolves.

"He's kind of a jerk," Kira lied. Truthfully, she'd kind of liked Nash. Even if he was presumptuous and forward with her. Hell, that was probably why she liked him. Kira had always liked her men strong. Really strong. There was nothing sexier than a man who knew what he wanted and was willing to go after it. And wasn't that the problem? Nash *was* sexy. Too sexy.

"Really?" Sasha walked with Kira toward the cabin. "That's too bad, but then again, we're used to dealing with Cranky Carl. He can't be worse than that, right?"

Kira shrugged. "I guess we'll see. Turns out Carl retired. Not that anyone bothered to tell me. But then again, why would they? I'm only supposed to be in charge around here. Speaking of which…" She turned to Sasha. "Shouldn't you be in the office?"

"Conner's in there. I needed a few minutes away. He's so foul these days. Maybe we can start calling him Cranky Conner?"

Kira resisted the urge to laugh. It would be a fitting name for the man whose attitude had only deteriorated since Kira was promoted to campground manager over him. But now that she was manager, more than ever, she needed to maintain some sort of professionalism and try to make peace with Conner.

"I'll have to have a talk with him," she said. "Especially if it's becoming a problem to work with him."

If Kira was looking for her friend to tell her it would be okay, she was definitely looking in the wrong place. Sasha shook her head, put her hands on her hips and looked Kira straight in the eye. "It's not going to be a problem. I'm sorry. I'm not trying to be a whiney employee or make trouble when there isn't any, but he's so hard to work with, Kira. I'll do my best with him but he's going to need to sort himself out, or I'm going to tell him how to—"

"No." Kira held her hand up. "I don't think there's any need to tell Conner anything." At least not what Sasha wanted to tell him, which no doubt would only put him in a worse mood, or put Kira in the middle of a very unfortunate argument. "I'll handle it, okay?"

Sasha nodded, satisfied for the moment, and Kira put dealing with Conner on her to-do list. *Right under dealing with the Nash situation.* Not that it was a situation, but it would be if she didn't deal with it. There was no way she was going to have a *wolf* working with her. Not in her campground. *Especially not one as sexy as—no.* It had nothing to do with his sex appeal. At least that's what she'd have to keep telling herself.

Kira sighed and refocused on her friend. "Take your break early then. I'll take over in the office and if I get the chance, I'll talk to Conner, okay?"

Sasha skipped off in the direction of the staff housing, and Kira resisted the urge to go with her. The promotion from last summer had been unexpected, and not necessarily what she would have chosen for herself, but it was a good job and considering she didn't have a whole lot of other choices—like going home—she needed to make the best of it. If that meant making some hard decisions and having some even harder conversations, that's just what she would do. But it didn't mean she had to like it.

Kira was just about to go inside the camp office when a green truck pulling into the staff parking lot stopped her. *Nash.*

She waited and watched while he hopped out of the cab, grabbed a duffel bag from the box of his truck and headed toward the south cabin.

Her cabin.

Oh hell no.

Of course, if Nash was the new resident handyman, he'd need a place to stay and although the thought had crossed her mind, she certainly hadn't considered the fact that he'd take the spare room in the south cabin, where she stayed. Employee lodging was co-ed, and generally the rooms were assigned based on availability. *Surely there must be another vacant room in one of the other cabins?*

Kira's entire body stiffened, and she did her best to ignore the surge of desire that had shot through her at the idea of only a thin wall separating Nash's bed from hers. *No.* She could not allow herself to feel anything for him. He was a wolf, for goodness' sake.

An incredibly hot wolf, the little voice in her head chimed in.

As if he sensed her, Nash chose that moment to turn and see Kira watching him.

Even from a distance, she could see the flash of his teeth as he grinned at her, the heat in his eyes. *No.* She turned away and slammed the office door against the wall as she opened it and went inside. She had a phone call to make. Because there was *no* way she could have Nash in such close proximity.

Nash knew he should probably back off when it came to Kira. Especially considering she'd turned out to be his boss. Sort of. Either way, she was the manager of the campground, and even if he didn't report directly to her, it probably wouldn't be a good idea to piss her off.

But even though he knew logically he shouldn't push her so hard, he couldn't stop himself. From the moment he'd laid eyes on those curves and thick, juicy lips, he knew he wouldn't rest until he'd had a taste of her. At the very least.

The moment he'd opened the door and hopped out of the truck, he'd sensed her. There was no mistaking her scent. She was delicious. Her animal was faint, but it was there. As if she'd been denying or neglecting it. He knew she stood there watching him, because even if she tried to pretend it didn't exist, there was no mistaking the scent of desire. Kira was definitely not going to come to it easily, and that would be half the fun, but she wanted him just as bad as he wanted her. They both felt it. Of that, Nash had no doubt.

Finally, he turned and grinned at her. Just as he expected, she turned and walked inside. He let her go. For now.

She would be a challenge, that was for sure. But if there was one thing Nash liked, it was a challenge. Especially one in the form of a feisty she-bear. He'd never been with a bear. Hell, he'd never even considered it. In his pack, the focus was on breeding and expanding the population.

When wolves had been reintroduced to Yellowstone in 1995, it had been controversial among the shifter community. Not everyone thought it was a good idea. Packs were divided and families split. Nash's family was pro-reintroduction and as a pack, they'd made it a priority to make the program successful. Which, for Nash and his brother meant mating and breeding with other wolves to further the population. No exceptions. If it wasn't a priority to find a suitable mate, there was no room in the pack for you.

It's not that Nash was against mating with another wolf. Not at all. He just didn't think it should be forced upon him. His brother, the alpha, disagreed. When Nash refused to accept the female Nolan had chosen for him, he'd been cast out. Not that those were the exact words Nolan used.

"Take some time, Nash," he said. "Get it out of your system, whatever it is. And when you're ready, come home, take a mate and do the right thing."

The right thing. Whatever that was.

And that was the problem. Nash and Nolan had very

different opinions on what exactly that was.

Nash walked into the cabin he'd been assigned and pushed thoughts of Nolan to the back of his mind. He was going to take the summer off, just the way his brother had suggested, and maybe when the seasons changed again, he might feel differently about his future. It was doubtful, but for his family, his pack, he'd give it a shot. Nash wasn't ready to completely close the door on his family. He knew what his decisions would mean for his future as well as his pack. And he still wasn't sure he was ready to turn his back on everything he'd ever known.

"Hey. You must be Nash."

A woman appeared in what looked to be the direction of the kitchen and smiled at him. She was petite, with deep-brown eyes and creamy dark skin that reminded Nash of a rich cup of hot chocolate.

"I am." He smiled at the beauty and offered his hand. "And you are?"

"Sasha. I work in the office. Welcome to Riverside."

"Thank you, Sasha." He dropped his bag at his feet and leaned against the wall next to her. She smelled floral and feminine. And human. Very different from Kira's earthy fresh scent. "It's good to be here. I'm looking forward to settling in. Do you happen to know which room is mine?"

"I'd be happy to show you."

She was cute, that was for sure, but Nash didn't feel the tug of arousal when he looked at her. "Oh, I'm sure you have work to do," he said smoothly. "I can find it." *There was only one female he wanted showing him any kind of bedroom.*

Sasha didn't bother hiding her disappointment. "It's the last room on the right." She pointed to a small hallway. "There's only two rooms over there, so you'll see it."

"And who has the other room?" He picked up his duffel. "Anything I should know about my neighbor?"

"That's Kira's room."

"Kira?" *Things were getting more and more interesting.*

"Yup. I think there's an extra room in the other cabin, if you'd rather—"

"No." Nash let a smile take over his face. "This is perfect." He started to walk in the direction she'd pointed. "I'll get settled and I'm sure I'll see you later, Sasha." He shot her one last smile and went to unpack.

CHAPTER THREE

"But I don't think you understand." Kira tried again to explain to the human resources woman that Nash wasn't a suitable hire for the Riverside campground, but the woman cut her off again.

"I understand perfectly," the woman said. "But just because you have a personality clash, as you put it, I can't fire him."

It was more than a personality clash. A lot more. It had been three days since Nash came to Riverside and into her life. Three days, where every time she saw him, her entire body reacted so violently, she could have sworn she was coming down with the flu or something. But it wasn't as simple as a virus or a bug she could fight off because whenever Nash wasn't around, she felt perfectly fine. But when he was close by, even in the same general area, her skin felt as though it were on fire and everything inside her strained to get out, as if she were going to burst.

Or shift.

That was it. Never in her entire life had she been more aware of the bear inside her. Even when she was a teenager and her hormones were all over the map, it hadn't felt like this. As if she were going to lose control at any moment. If she didn't know better, she would have thought that Nash was somehow connected to her, important to her and her bear in some way.

Except that didn't make any sense at all. *Why would a wolf be connected to a bear?* She was a grizzly, for God's sake. They didn't even particularly like the wolf packs in Montana, where she grew up. There was definitely no connection to them.

Of any kind.

Whatever was going on, all Kira knew was that it had something to do with Nash and it was starting to jeopardize how she could do her job. If she was always worried about being in close proximity to Nash—or God forbid, alone with him—there was no telling what could happen. But whatever it was that *might* happen, it couldn't. Not in front of anyone.

Which was why she was on the phone with human resources, trying to get Nash moved to another campground, or anything really. But she didn't want him fired. That wasn't fair.

The woman on the other end was still talking about the legal ramifications of what it would mean if she let him go without cause, or something to that effect. She couldn't be sure, because she mostly stopped listening until there was a pause and Kira sighed. The conversation was moving in circles.

"I'm not asking you to fire him," she said, trying not to let the frustration creep into her voice. "I just think maybe he'd be better suited at one of the other campgrounds."

"No," the woman said again. "I'm unable to move his position unless he'd done something that gives grounds for firing. Has he done anything you need to report to me?"

"No." Kira wasn't prepared to go so far as to have Nash fired. And there was no way she could properly convey her reasons for wanting him moved to a different campground. Not to the HR woman on the other end of the phone, anyway. It's not as if she could tell her he was really a wolf and he was sexy as hell and presented all kinds of dangers to her, not the least of which was the way he made her feel. *No. She couldn't say any of that.* "It's fine," Kira said after a moment. "Sorry I bothered you."

She hung up the phone in her office and dropped her head into her hands. She was stuck with him. Kira dug her thumbs into her temples. Not that it was the worst thing that could happen. It wasn't. She just needed to get a handle on herself. And mostly why she felt so strongly about getting rid of him when she couldn't stop thinking about him.

Maybe *that* was the problem? No. That was *definitely* the problem.

She pressed her fingers deeper and muttered, "The last thing I need right now is a bloody wolf."

"What wolf?"

Kira dropped her hands and shot up in her seat to see Conner in the doorway of her tiny office. She hadn't heard him knock. *How much had he heard?* She seriously needed to stop talking out loud.

"Is there a wolf in the campground?"

She could have sworn she saw him try to hold back a smile. No doubt he'd like it if there was a wolf problem. Anything to make it harder for her to do her job and give him the opportunity to rub it in her face that he should have been promoted instead of her. She'd spoken to him, just like she'd promised Sasha she would, but it clearly hadn't made much of a difference to his attitude.

"No," she said quickly and stood, straightening her shirt as she did so. "I was just thinking of a book I'd read."

He didn't look as though he believed her, but that was

23

his problem.

"Did you need something, Conner?"

He nodded and crossed his arms over his chest and scowled. He would have been handsome if he wasn't so damn bitter all the time. "I just got an interesting complaint from a camper in site 25."

"Did you file it? I can take a look in—"

"I think you'll want to look at it now."

Something in his voice caught her attention. It was more than Conner being grumpy or angry. "Is everything okay?"

He shook his head, genuine concern in his eyes. "I'm not sure. But the man, a Mr...." He consulted a piece of paper in his hands. "Brantly. Mr. Brantly reported some dead fish on the riverbanks while he was out fishing with his son. Said he wouldn't have thought anything of it except there were about five of them in one spot and they're right out front of his site, so of course he was worried about the smell. He wasn't sure if he should report it or not, but his wife thought he should let us know."

Dead fish? It was unusual for sure. The rivers in Yellowstone were some of the best fisheries around. Certainly, every once in a while, there'd be some sort of disease or natural occurrence that caused a disruption. It wasn't common but there hadn't been anything issued from the head office. "That does sound..."

"Fishy?" Connor laughed at his own joke, but Kira only rolled her eyes.

"I was going to say, strange. Site 25 you said?" Conner nodded. "Thanks for letting me know. Make sure you make note if any other reports come in. I'll go check it out and clean it up."

"Oh, don't worry," Conner said. "I ran into the new maintenance guy. He said he'd take care of it."

"Nash?" Her body tensed.

"That's him."

She grabbed the keys to her ATV and stuffed them in her pocket before she reached for her field bag. "I better go check anyway. It definitely sounds strange." She tried to be as casual as possible as she moved past Conner. "Thanks again for letting me know."

She'd only been in charge of the Riverside campground for less than a month. It wouldn't look good if she already had things going wrong and she couldn't afford to lose the job. She'd been lucky to get it after that jerk Ryan Dixon showed his true colors and admitted to using her. He'd left her like yesterday's garbage, right before his entire clan moved on. Embarrassed and heartbroken, she'd curled up in a tent and cried for days before finally pulling herself together long enough to come up with a plan. Not that it was much of one. Ashamed, alone, and out of options, she took the first job she could find. It wasn't home, but it wasn't bad either and she wasn't going to let something as small as a few dead fish screw things up just as she was getting back on her feet again.

She jammed the keys into the ignition of the ATV and fired it up, letting the roar of the engine drown out her real concern. Because it wasn't a few dead fish that she was *really* worried about.

It was a wolf.

He'd lived in Yellowstone half of his life and Nash had never seen anything like the pile of dead trout on the side of the riverbank. He'd just finished putting his few belongings away when he'd run into Conner. Truthfully, he'd been looking for Kira but when the other man told him about the dead fish, he'd volunteered right away to go check it out.

It was strange. No, it was downright suspicious. And from what he could tell from the fish, whatever had killed them, it hadn't been natural.

With a sigh, he looked at the fish he held in his gloved hand and tossed it into the bucket at his feet. "Such a shame," he muttered. If there was something that made Nash mad, it was when the resources of the land he loved were wasted or damaged. Whatever it was killing the fish, he was definitely going to find out.

He left the bucket and walked a little farther down the shore, keeping his eye out for more fish, when the hairs on the back of his neck stood up. *Kira.*

She was close. He could feel it. His entire body thrummed in a way that was both unusual and familiar all at once. He couldn't remember the last time he'd been so aware of a female. Which was likely because he'd *never* been so aware. Not like this. He stopped walking and waited until she turned off her ATV and caught up with him. He turned as she came up behind him.

Kira started. He could see her tense.

"I heard you drive up," he said as way of explanation. It's not as though he could tell her that he'd sensed her. That he *felt* her just as he felt the blood pump through his veins. She was already clearly unhappy with his presence; Nash was definitely not going to freak her out with that little piece of information. "Connor told you about the fish?"

She nodded and pointed to the bucket. "You didn't have to do that."

"It was no big thing." He shrugged. "Besides, I'm the maintenance guy. It's what I do."

"Still." She shook her head, but he could see the concern lining her face as she looked at the pile of dead trout in the bucket. "You...wow. There are a lot of them, aren't there?" Kira crouched next to the bucket and pulled a pair of gloves from her back pocket. He couldn't help being impressed as she picked up a fish with none of the squeamishness of most of the women he knew. "What do you think happened?"

Nash squatted next to her, so close he could feel the heat from her body. To keep from touching her, he picked up a fish of his own and examined it despite the fact he'd already looked at each one of them and couldn't see anything unusual. "I've been racking my brain, trying to figure it out, but it just doesn't make sense. The only thing—"

"It was a rhetorical question," Kira snapped.

"Okay." Nash tossed the dead fish back in with the others and stood. His instincts might be going wild for this woman but that didn't mean he needed to stick around while she snapped at him. "I was just trying to help. But if you got it all figured out, boss. By all means." He held up his hands and took a few steps backward before she got to her feet.

"Nash, I..."

"You're what?" He tried not to grin but he could see the apology would be hard for her.

"I appreciate you cleaning up the mess."

It took him a second to realize she hadn't apologized for anything after all. "You appreciate it?"

She nodded. "I do. Thank you."

"That's it?"

"Was there something else?"

Damn this woman.

She wasn't going to apologize for snapping at him and being rude for no reason at all except she was clearly struggling with the way she was feeling about him. Because

27

she was feeling something. Of that much, Nash was sure. More than that, the sexy as hell she-bear had no idea that despite the fact that she'd been nothing but rude to him from the moment they'd met, all he was trying to do was help her out. What he should have done was walk away, maybe even told her off and put her in her place before leaving her to figure out her dead fish on her own.

But he couldn't. And he wouldn't.

In fact, he *should* have done a lot of things that would have made a lot more sense than what he was about to do.

A deep growl threatened to escape his throat and in that moment, Nash knew he had no other choice. He'd been drawn to her in a way that went far beyond him and what he was in control of.

His actions were pure instinct as he took two long, smooth strides toward her so he stood barely an inch from her. She was tall but he still had height on her, and when she looked up at him with fire flaring in the dark depths of her eyes, what was left of his control evaporated.

"You need to be taught some manners, Kira."

"Pardon me?"

Before she could say another word, Nash bent and scooped her up as if she weighed little more than his duffel bag. Her fists flung out at him, but he dodged her blows easily and positioned her over his shoulder before he pinned her in place with one strong arm.

"Put me down!"

"No."

A sense of calm that he hadn't felt since he'd arrived a few days earlier, and her sexy ass had walked into that campground shower, washed through him. He walked toward the river.

"Nash! Put me down right now!"

"No."

"So help me..." He held her tighter with his arm, enjoying the feel of her ample breasts pressed against his back, the core of her squirming against his shoulder. It was a feeling he could get used to. Not that she would let him carry her around again. *But, you never knew what could happen...*

Nash strode into the river until the water, still icy from the mountain runoff, hit the top of his thighs. The cold water did nothing to dampen his desire, but he knew it would have the desired effect on Kira. Before she realized what his intentions were, Nash released his grip on Kira and dumped her into the rushing water.

He would *not* do it!

By the time Kira's brain caught up with her body, and she realized that not only *would* Nash dump her in the water, he *had* just done it, it was too late to form any other thought. All she could see was a haze of red anger in her vision as she splashed and sputtered in the cold river.

Fortunately for Nash, the river flowed fast enough that Kira moved quickly downstream from where he'd so unceremoniously dumped her. If she'd surfaced, sputtering and pissed off, anywhere within striking range of him, he wouldn't be standing there with that grin that, at that particular moment, looked a whole lot more annoying than it did sexy.

"What the hell, Nash?" Kira hoisted herself up and gained her footing in the quick-moving water. "Are you trying to lose your job?"

His grin only got bigger if it was possible, and with a ridiculously quick stride, he closed some of the distance between them. But not all of it; he was smarter than that. "If you could take my job, you would have done it already.

Am I right?"

Kira clenched her hands into fists at her side. Water dripped down her face. *Damn him for seeing right through her. Damn him for getting to her. And damn him for knowing there wasn't a goddamn thing she could do about it.* What was more, the icy water had done nothing to erase the surge of desire that had been pulsing through her body from the moment he picked her up and pressed her against his shoulder.

Dammit.

Afraid she'd say something that would give her away, Kira took a moment, ran her hands through her hair, pasting the wet strands against her head, in an attempt to regain as much composure as she could before she turned and attempted to gracefully stalk out of the river to the opposite bank. It would take her farther away from the camp office, into the woods, but there was no way she was going to go back to face her staff when she was soaking wet. Especially not considering Nash would most certainly be right behind her and more than willing to tell the tale of how she'd ended up that way.

No way.

"The office is that way."

"I know exactly where the office is," Kira spat over her shoulder. Her boot slipped on a rock and she almost went face-first back into the river but Nash's strong hand on her upper arm held her fast. She straightened up and shook him off. "Let go of me."

"I was just trying to help."

Kira stepped quickly out of the river and onto the safety of the bank before she spun around to face him. "Really? Is that what you were doing by throwing me into the river? *Helping* me? Because if you were, you have a pretty messed up way of showing it."

Before he could respond, she turned and stalked into

the trees.

He didn't say anything, but Kira could feel his nearness. Her entire body was ice-cold from the water. *So why did her skin feel as though it were burning up? What was it about this wolf?* She needed to get farther away. She needed to get as far away from him as she could. If she shifted into her bear, she might be able to outrun him, or at the very least challenge him. There was no way a wolf would be able to go up against a grizzly. Not even one as cocky and arrogant as Nash.

But she wasn't going to shift. There was no point and it would only do more harm than good in the long run. Besides, she'd decided months ago to stop even attempting to get in touch with her bear.

And her brother.

She wouldn't even try to deny that after leaving Ryan and his clan, shifting into her animal had more to do with trying to reconnect with her twin brother and her clan back home than anything else. It had *everything* to do with that.

But she wouldn't. Not anymore.

The only way to get rid of this asshole would be to confront him. Anger welled up inside her to the point Kira thought she might explode. As soon as she was in the protection of the pines, she whirled around to face him.

"Leave me alone." She forced the words out through gritted teeth.

His lips flicked up into what might have been the start of a smile. Fortunately, he was smart enough to stifle it, or Kira would have wiped it right off his face.

"I'm not trying to piss you off, Kira."

He almost sounded genuine. Maybe he was, but she was definitely not in the mood to figure it out either way. But something about his voice stopped her. Or maybe she was just tired of being mad and trying to keep this feeling from completely consuming her. Either way, the fight sank out of her and she dropped her hands to her sides.

"Then why are you following me? Just leave me alone." She bit the inside of her cheek to keep from crying. The very last thing she wanted to do was show any kind of weakness to Nash. She'd learned to swallow her tears very early on, growing up with three brothers. "I just want to be alone."

Nash took a step toward her. "I don't believe that."

She shook her head. "I don't care what you—"

"I think you do." He took another step closer but she didn't back away. "I think you care a lot about what I think."

It was such a strange and intimate thing for him to say. Especially considering from the moment they'd met, she'd tried to push him away.

Maybe that was why? Maybe Nash knew exactly what had been going through her head from the moment Kira had laid eyes on him.

He reached out; his fingers wrapped around a thick, wet strand of hair that had escaped her braid. He tucked it behind her ear. At that exact moment, a flood of heat pooled between her legs. Kira's knees almost buckled from the intensity of the simple touch and the explosion of sensation it caused within her.

She squeezed her eyes shut and tried to shake her head, but his hand cupped around her cheek.

"Kira—"

"No." She struggled to keep her breath slow and even. His proximity was wreaking havoc with her. She'd never experienced anything like it. Not even with Ryan, and he'd been her fated mate. At least that's what she'd thought before he'd dumped her and left her with nowhere to go.

"Kira." Nash's voice was as tender as his touch had

been. "Look at me."

Despite herself, she did. His steely, gray eyes were inches from her. So close that she could see there were flecks of black and green in them. Like marbles. They were captivating, and they were staring directly into her soul.

"I'm sorry I threw you in the river." He spoke softly and she believed him. "I just wanted you to stop for one minute and see that I'm not the enemy."

"You're a wolf."

The corner of his mouth flicked up into a slow smile that caused another wave of desire to crash through her. "I'm aware."

"I'm a bear."

"Again," he said. "I'm aware."

"That's...it..."

"What?"

What? How could he even ask that? How could such a casual question come out of his mouth when it was so obvious? He was a wolf. She was a bear. Two very separate and distinct species and although Kira honestly didn't know how it worked in Yellowstone, where she came from, that was a problem. A real one.

"I like you, Kira." His words sent a sizzle through her veins. "And I get the feeling you might like me, too." His eyes danced with mischief. "At least a little."

She swallowed hard. There was no point denying anything. Not when it was so obvious to both of them. "That doesn't mean it's okay," she said instead.

"Says who?" Nash took a step back and held his arms out. "Is there anyone around here telling us it's a problem?" He spun in a slow circle. And then faster. "Hello?" he called out, his voice laced with laughter. "Does anyone out there object to a wolf and a bear being friends?"

Kira jumped at him and clasped her hand over his

mouth. "Quiet."

"Who's going to hear?" Nash laughed and removed her hand, holding it in his. "We're in the middle of the forest."

For the first time, she looked around. They'd walked a lot farther than she'd intended. Kira always had underestimated how fast she could travel when her emotions were heated. And he was right; there was no one around to hear them. She'd really noticed that about Yellowstone. At least around the main campgrounds, the tourists stuck pretty close to the public areas and didn't venture off the beaten track very much. The park services group did a good job drilling it into everyone's head that the animals were wild and their area should be protected. Ultimately, it led to a lot of privacy, as far as shifters were concerned. And at that very moment, it meant that Kira and Nash were very much alone.

Her hand was still in his. The touch that should have been so simple was lighting her up and causing all of her senses to go haywire.

"In fact," Nash said. "If I kissed you right now," he tugged her closer, "no one would ever know." His lips were so close to hers she could feel the warm puffs of air when he spoke.

"We'd know," she said in a lame attempt to deter his advances.

He licked his lips. "Oh baby, I guarantee we'll know. And it won't be something either of us will forget anytime soon."

Nash's free hand cupped the back of her head and pulled her into him until her lips crushed against his. There was nothing soft or tentative about the kiss. It was all passion and need, and it only took a second before Kira's hands found his shoulders, pulling him even closer into her.

His tongue pushed between her lips, exploring her mouth, twisting together with hers. She moaned, or maybe it was him. She couldn't be sure and she didn't care because it was the single best kiss she'd ever had.

For a moment—a long, delicious moment—she let herself fall into the sensation of it all. But when it got to be too much, Kira put an end to it.

She stepped back, pulling herself just far enough away from him that she could pull in a deep breath. Her fingers went to her lips. Confusion raced through her.

Neither of them spoke for a few seconds. *At least it wasn't just her who was trying to regain her composure.* Nash was clearly just as affected by their kiss as she'd been.

Finally, he spoke first. "I knew there was something," he said. "But...you...damn. You have every natural instinct inside me going crazy, woman."

"Instinct?" She shook her head. That couldn't be right. "But you're a wolf."

"I thought we already established that." His cocky grin was back, but he softened it by grabbing her hand. "And you're a grizzly. Remember?"

She tried not to smile. "But then how can your instincts be doing anything?" Kira shook her head, aware she wasn't making any sense. "I mean...us...this." She gestured between them. "It's just—"

"It's just whatever we decide it is," he finished for her. "Why don't we just leave it at that for now because I think we can both agree that there's something between us—am I right? I mean, I don't know about you, Kira, but bear or not, I've never shared a kiss like that before and I'd be more than happy for a replay."

Leave it at that? Could she? Could she just stop thinking about the fact that he was a wolf and she was a bear and just let how she was feeling rule the moment?

Nash leaned forward, pressed his lips against hers again and the decision was made.

Hell yes. At least for the time being, if it meant more kisses like that one, she could definitely let things between them just be *whatever.*

CHAPTER FOUR

Nash drove the nail into the two-by-four with only a few swings of his hammer before he moved on to the next one. He was on autopilot. Not that repairing a few broken picnic tables took a whole lot of brainpower. And it was a good thing, too, because the only thing he'd been able to think of for the last twenty-four hours was that kiss.

The kiss.

Damn.

It's not as if it had been a stretch to imagine what kissing Kira would be like. The moment he saw her, he'd seen it. She was teeming with sensuality. The kind that she didn't even know she was hiding from herself.

But even though he'd known it would be hot as hell, Nash had not been prepared for the reality of it. And now, it was all he could do to concentrate on the simple task of hammering a few nails; all he could think of was laying Kira down on one of the tables he was fixing and showing her exactly how hot that kiss had been and what he intended to do about it. Because he did intend to do something about it. Just as soon as he had even the slightest chance to get her alone.

That was the problem. They were never alone. If Nash

thought that having the room directly next to hers in the tiny staff cabin they shared was going to afford him any time with Kira, he'd been wrong. Very wrong. A constant stream of people milled about the cabin, at literally all hours. Nash hadn't even thought that many people worked at the Riverside campground. And truth be told, they probably didn't. Staff throughout Yellowstone had a habit of traveling around the park on their days off and crashing wherever they could. Not that it mattered. Where there was a will, there was very much a way and Nash definitely had the desire to get Kira alone. Soon.

First, he had a job to do. As monotonous as repairing picnic tables was, Nash had chosen the task that afternoon with the distinct purpose of losing himself in physical labor. If anything could take the edge off his need and his animal straining at the very edge of control, it was working up a good sweat.

He finished with the table he was working on, propped his hammer up on the bucket of nails and easily lifted the table with only the slightest strain on his biceps. He carried it over to one side and grabbed the next one. He was alone behind the maintenance shack, but he should probably use a bit more judgment when it came to using his strength so openly. He wasn't usually so reckless. But that's because he didn't usually feel as though he were on the edge of exploding. His wolf wanted out in a fierce way and the sensation was only getting stronger. Especially when he was around Kira

Nash knew exactly what it meant. *She was his.*

He needed her. The fact that she was a bear and he was a wolf— a *Yellowstone* wolf—didn't matter. Not to his animal. The only thing that mattered was quenching the fire inside.

Nash let a growl slip from his throat and he picked up

the hammer again, determined to focus his energies on something he actually could control.

"What exactly are people thinking when they stand on these things," he muttered and grabbed a nail from the bucket. "They're thinking they're on holidays and they're not going to have to worry about fixing it, so might as well," he answered himself and swung the hammer, hitting the nail into the board.

It was an easy fix. Most of them were, and before long, he'd repaired all the broken tables. He was in the shack, replacing his tools, when his cell phone rang. His heart leapt until he realized Kira didn't have his number. She would have used the radios if she wanted to get a hold of him. He almost ignored the phone altogether. And as soon as he looked at the number, he wished he would have.

With a sigh, he answered his older brother's call.

"Nolan."

"Oh, you answered this time. I feel honored."

Nash bit back a sharp retort. There was no point engaging him. Besides, there was a reason Nash didn't answer his brother's calls, and they both knew it. "What do you need, Nolan?"

"You know exactly what I need, Nash."

He rolled his eyes, thankful his brother couldn't see him. Nash was a strong alpha male, but Nolan was too. The difference between them was that Nash had the sense to know it wasn't worth it. Beyond some roughhousing when they were younger, the North brothers had never engaged in a real fight. And Nash had no plans to change that, because when two alpha males clashed, it never ended well. One of them would end up seriously injured. Or worse. Which was why Nash had left the pack.

Leaving everything and everyone he knew and loved was preferable to the alternative.

"I need to know if you're done screwing around, Nash. The pack needs you."

"The pack doesn't need me." He finished tidying up the workbench and flicked out the light behind him. "You only think they do."

"Bullshit. You know as well as I do why the pack needs you. Come home."

Nash shook his head. "You know I can't, big brother. Not unless you're cool with my choices."

"Your choices?" Nolan all but growled into the phone. "Or your *lack* of choices?"

It always came back to the same argument for Nolan. He wanted Nash to choose a mate. That was why he had to leave. Nolan didn't understand that he wasn't about to pick a mate from a lineup, as if he were ordering up a new living room set. It was ridiculous. Just because Nolan thought that was an acceptable way to find a mate didn't mean Nash did. Not even a little bit. Especially considering he saw firsthand how miserable his big brother was since mating with Julia. She was beautiful. And she was a pure wolf from a solid pack, which no doubt was all Nolan had needed to know before choosing her. But there was emptiness in her eyes and it was easy to see she was every bit as unhappy as Nolan was.

Pure bloodlines weren't everything. There was no way Nash was going to put himself through that. He was not about to sign up for a lifetime of misery for the sole purpose of procreating.

There was more to life.

There was Kira.

Not that he was about to explain that to Nolan.

"I've made my choice, brother." Nash stepped out of the shack, into the late afternoon sunshine. The days were warming quickly and before long, the heat of the summer would be upon them. "I'm not taking a mate of your choice just because someone thinks I should."

"You know exactly how important it is to our kind to increase the population, Nash." He could almost see the vein in his brother's forehead bulging. "It wasn't all that long ago that we were completely wiped out of Yellowstone. Our ancestors were lucky to escape. You know that."

"Yeah, I know that." *Did he ever know that.* It was all anyone in his pack talked about. The ancestors and how they'd been slaughtered and driven out of the park. The ones who stayed had to hide their wolves, shutting off that part of themselves, some taking human mates and basically breeding the wolf out of them. Some, like Nash and Nolan's parents, successfully hid their wolf side and worked tirelessly for the reintroduction. From what Nash heard, there were still a few of the *originals* in the park. Not that it mattered now that the reintroduction had happened.

"Our people worked and sacrificed for years to get back to our land, Nash. The least we can do is help build numbers, reestablish a presence in Yellowstone the way it's supposed to be. It's our duty."

There it was. That word.

Nash sighed. The irony was, he would have had no problem staying with the pack if Nolan hadn't gotten it into his head that their mates had to be *pure* and from specific packs. If he could have been left alone to fall in love and choose his own mate, everything would have been fine. But, as he was reminded more than once, that wasn't the way it worked.

"It's not my duty, Nolan. If you choose to be unhappy for the rest of your life because your mate feels more like a piece of property than a partner, that's your choice, but I'm not—"

"You'll do what I tell you," his brother roared into the phone. He'd pissed off Nolan before, but he'd never heard him quite so angry. "If you ever want to set foot within a hundred yards of our land again, you will *choose* a suitable mate, brother."

That sounded an awful lot like an ultimatum. And it rocked him.

They'd had their disagreements, and yes, Nash left. But he never thought he wouldn't be able to return. Home was home. Nolan had never told him he wouldn't be welcome back.

"Did you hear me?"

Nash nodded. "I heard you."

"It's for the good of the pack, Nash."

"Right. The pack."

The sound of an ATV coming, followed moments later by Kira's fresh sexy scent, filled his senses and distracted him just enough so he didn't tell Nolan what he really thought about the good of the pack.

"Nash, I know you don't see it right now, but—"

"I can't talk right now." He cut him off as Kira's ATV pulled up next to his truck. Before his brother said another word, he disconnected the call and stuffed his phone into his back pocket.

"Hey."

Kira felt like a teenager, the way his voice and one simple word made her knees wobble. It was ridiculous. What was even more ridiculous was that she brushed her hair, refastened her braid, and brushed her teeth before she drove out to the maintenance shed to see Nash. But she hadn't been able to stop thinking about him and that kiss. *Yes.* That kiss had definitely been the star of her dreams the night before, and a whole lot more.

Wolf or not, the man knew how to kiss. Of that, there was no doubt.

"Hey yourself." *Did she really say that? When had she turned into some sort of love struck girlie girl?* She shook her head and tried again. "How's it going?" *That was better.* Maybe she could actually have a conversation without it turning into her making a fool of herself.

Nash crossed the distance between them and without saying another word, cupped his hand around the back of her head and pulled her into him. He kissed her hard and fast, leaving the promise for more. Much more. But then it was done. He pulled away and Kira opened her eyes.

She hadn't realized she'd closed them.

"It's going a lot better now," he said. "I've been thinking about that all day."

"I have...I mean...we probably shouldn't do that where people might see."

Why had she just said that? With the way the blood raced through her body and the damp heat had settled between her legs, Kira was pretty sure she didn't care whether anyone saw them. She wanted more. She *needed* more and judging by her internal turmoil, her bear clearly agreed.

"Isn't that why you're here?" Nash reached for her hand and laced his fingers through hers. "It's pretty private here."

It *was* private there, which was exactly why Kira had decided to drive out to see Nash instead of calling him over the radio. But admitting that little fact at that moment probably wasn't a great idea because it could only lead down one path. And as turned on as she was, she was still a bear and he was still a wolf and nothing could happen between them. Besides the fact that the last man she'd put her trust in had betrayed her in an epic fashion, Kira was more than a little gun-shy. Yet she couldn't seem to fight the pull Nash had over her.

"It's actually not why I'm here." She forced herself to focus. "There was a report of more dead fish earlier today."

"What? Let's go. I'll help you—"

"I took care of it." His lips pressed into a line. "Mostly," she added.

"You know I would have helped you," he said. "You shouldn't have to clean that up on your own. Besides, there's something not right about those fish. Next time, I'd like the chance to check it out."

Kira smiled. "You might just get that chance. I have a theory and I was hoping you'd help me out with it." She'd been hoping he'd help her out with a lot more than the dead fish problem, but that wasn't the point.

Nash nodded to the shack. "I have some water inside. Come on in and tell me what you need."

Kira followed him, but waited outside on one of the picnic tables while Nash retrieved a few bottles of water and brought them back out. She drank half of hers before she told him what she'd been thinking about. "There were six more dead fish this morning," she started. "And they were in almost the same spot as before. Strange, right?"

"Very."

"Don't you think if there was something in the water killing the fish that we'd be finding them all over the riverbank? Not just in that one spot?"

Nash shrugged. "Probably. Maybe it has something to do with that location? Like a geothermal opening or something."

Kira shook her head. She had a different idea. "I mean, a geothermal opening isn't totally out of the question, but I have a different theory. And I was hoping you'd help me out with it. Tonight."

That caught his attention. He tilted his head and stared deep into her eyes. *Oh yes, she was in trouble.*

"You know I will."

There was a lot more meaning behind his words. Kira swallowed hard and picked up her water bottle again. "Great." She tipped it back and finished the rest in a desperate attempt to cool off. "We'll leave about eleven, okay?"

"Sounds good to me."

She stood to leave because Kira knew if she stuck around too much longer, she'd probably leap across the table and kiss him again. *Lord knew she couldn't stop staring at those lips and imagining exactly how they'd feel moving against the tender skin of her neck, traveling up to the shell of her ear where—*

"I should go."

Kira straightened her khakis and turned away from him in an effort to maintain some sort of semblance of self-control. It was one thing to kiss him as a greeting, which they totally shouldn't have done. Or invite him on a middle-of-the-night stakeout, or whatever it was that she was planning on doing beyond getting him alone in the middle of the night. But it was a completely different thing to jump the man and push him down on the picnic table so she could straddle him and feel that hard muscular chest under her— *Oh good God.* She needed to get out of there. She quickened her step.

"Hey, Kira?" Nash called out to her. She almost didn't turn around, but there was something in the playful way he said her name. Despite her intentions to make a clean getaway, she turned to look at him. "I'm looking forward to tonight." His words melted off his tongue. They might as well have had a direct line between her legs because just the anticipation of later, and knowing he was looking forward to it as much as she was, made her panties wet.

CHAPTER FIVE

Kira hadn't given him many details about what exactly they were going to be doing out in the dark on the riverbank. Not that Nash needed any. He was quite happy to finally have a few moments alone with her. Especially at night, in the woods. The fact that they were supposed to be looking into her theory about the dead fish bared little importance to Nash. All he could think of was: Kira, alone, woods.

Perfect.

If only they could get out of the cabin.

"I'm not doing anything." Sasha sidled up to Nash and leaned up against the counter next to him. "Maybe I should come with you."

"No." Kira appeared in the hall. "What I meant to say was, I appreciate the offer, Sasha, but I think it's only a two-person job tonight."

Nash hid his smile and reached past Sasha, who actually pouted a little, to grab a few apples from the bowl on the counter. Sasha was a very attractive woman and she hadn't done a very good job of hiding her interest in Nash since he'd arrived. Under different circumstances, Nash might have pursued something with her, even if it was just a little fun. But circumstances weren't different. Besides, he got the impression that Sasha might be interested in almost every other man in the camp as well. Not that it mattered. Not at all.

He let his gaze slide over to Kira, who wore jeans that hugged her curves in all the right places and a v-neck t-shirt that stretched tight over her luscious breasts. *Damn.* If he thought she looked hot in her parks uniform, she was set to combust in her after-hours clothes. Nash swallowed hard and forced himself to focus on packing a few snacks.

"How long will you guys be gone?" Sasha directed her question at Kira. "Should we wait up?" She wiggled her eyebrows, but Nash knew it was only to tease, and likely try to suss out whether or not there was anything going on between the two of them. *If she only knew.* But she wouldn't because they'd done a good job hiding whatever it was that was going on between them from the other staff. At least for now.

Not that Nash saw any point to it. But he wasn't about to pretend he understood women or what went through their heads. Especially Kira's.

"Probably all night," Nash answered Sasha's question. "And we should get going." He grabbed his pack, squeezed past Sasha and stood in front of Kira. Up close, her scent filled him, driving his wolf wild. "Are you ready?" The question was loaded and, judging by the look on her face, Kira knew it.

"Thanks for coming with me tonight." They'd been driving in Nash's truck for a few minutes before Kira finally spoke, beyond telling him what direction to go in. She knew she should say something, but everything felt awkward and staged. As if she'd invited him on a date instead of a stakeout. Which, maybe, she had. She risked a glance in his direction and immediately felt stupid when he caught her eye and smiled.

"Of course, Kira. I'm happy to be here."

"It's just that it's late and the middle of the—"

"I'm a wolf, remember?" He laughed. "I like the night."

She laughed at the easy way he opened up about his animal. It was refreshing to spend time with another shifter, even if he was a wolf. And even though for the last year, she'd largely ignored the fact that she herself was a shifter, it was still nice. Even if she couldn't fully put that feeling into words. Or any other feeling when it came to Nash. There were so many reasons she shouldn't be sitting next to him in that truck, driving into the quiet woods in the middle of the night. But there was one good reason that she should.

She felt the need of it. Of *him*. Deep in her bones. And she couldn't ignore it any more.

"Where are we headed?" Nash drew her back into the moment. "I'm all about surprises," he smiled, "but I do need to know where to go."

She laughed. Something she found herself doing more and more when Nash was around. "Sorry. I maybe should have given you some more details. I was thinking we could go set up a camp across the river from the campsite, and just upstream from where the fish have been showing up. I think it's strange and I'm sure someone is putting them there."

"I totally agree with you." Without further instructions, Nash took the turn that would take them away from camp and across the bridge where they could backtrack and get to the other side without being spotted. As they got closer, he cut the lights and made the rest of the way in the dark.

"I think this is good right here." She whispered and then

laughed at herself. "Do you want to stay here, or maybe come with me closer to the river?"

His hand reached across the cab and squeezed hers. "You know exactly where I want to be."

A shot of desire raced through her and straight to her core at his words. She forced a calmness into her voice and pulled her hand away. "Great. I brought a few things. I put them in the back. We should probably go and get set up so that if there is someone out there, we don't disturb them or scare them away."

She was a terrible actress, and there was no doubt Nash could see right through her, but she didn't know what else to do. She'd been putting him off from the moment they'd met, and she could tell herself it was because he was a wolf and she was a bear. Or that they worked together, or....well, anything really. Kira *could* keep convincing herself of all the reasons it wasn't right. Or she could just take a chance, throw reason out the window and just go with it.

Out of the two options, there was one clear winner.

Nash nodded slowly and for a moment, Kira was afraid he would call her out. Instead, he smiled. "Well, we should get going then."

She'd packed a small bag of blankets, both to sit on and to keep warm with. A thermos of coffee and a few snacks. It wasn't much, but then again she didn't plan to be out all night. With any luck, they'd see what they needed to right away, and catch the culprit she was so sure was behind the dead fish. Because it had to be a person. There was no way the fish were dying naturally.

They found a sheltered spot where they could sit side by side and each have a pine tree to lean up against. Kira poured them each a mug of coffee and settled in.

"Tell me something, Kira."

She paused, the mug halfway to her mouth. "What's that?" She took a sip of her coffee.

"Why are you fighting this so much when you're so clearly attracted to me?"

Kira almost spat out her coffee. Instead, she swallowed hard in an effort not to choke on the hot liquid. It took her a minute to regain her composure. A minute that Nash spent staring at her, waiting for an answer. "What makes you think I'm attracted to you?" It was a stupid comeback and they both knew it, so she followed it up with a more truthful response. Her shoulders sagged a little. "Because you're a wolf."

"I've noticed." He chuckled. "But beyond using it as an excuse, I didn't think you had. Noticed, I meant."

She spun to face him. "What do you mean? Of course I've noticed. You're cocky and arrogant and…"

"Sexy as hell?"

Kira groaned in frustration.

"Does that mean I'm right?"

She put her coffee down and dropped her head into her hands. "I don't know what you want me to say. Of course I've noticed you. And yes, you're sexy. Happy? I said it."

Kira looked up to see Nash shake his head. "No," he said simply. "I'm not happy because all I really want is for you to stop fighting me and this attraction that we so clearly have for each other." He reached across the distance and cupped her head. His thumb stroked her cheek and he moved closer, so he sat directly in front of her. "And don't try to deny that it's there," he said. "I know you feel it when I kiss you. I know you feel the same need I feel."

His mouth was only inches from hers. She could feel his breath and when he finally pressed his lips to hers, she thought she might totally combust with the need for him.

Greedily, her mouth pressed up in an effort to connect. He was right; she'd been fighting everything and for the life of her, with his hands on her body, his mouth on hers, and sparks of desire coursing between both of them, Kira could not remember why.

The stakeout was forgotten as her hands slid up his chest, working their way under his jacket and t-shirt to find the hard, smooth, chiseled stomach underneath. His skin was hot beneath her cool touch. Kira leaned back, and Nash adjusted her on the blanket until she lay down and he straddled her. His mouth left hers and moved down to the sensitive skin on her neck. He was gentle but demanding as he nipped and sucked. Her back arched and she pressed her hips into him.

The time for reasoning her feelings and needs away was gone. There was nothing but Nash, the heat he sparked in her, and the need she could no longer deny.

She tasted like honey and coffee and the most delicious confection Nash had ever had on his tongue. He wanted more. He needed more because another kiss was not going to be enough this time. He needed all of her.

The feel of her hands on his skin drove him wild, and his kiss deepened, tangling his tongue with hers. He settled her underneath him and moved his hands down to find the zipper of her coat. There were way too many clothes between them. The spring air had a chilling bite, but Nash doubted either of them would feel it. They were only focused on one thing: fulfilling the carnal desires that had a grip over both of them.

The teeth of the zipper caught, trapping her in her clothing. Nash growled, and fought the urge to tear the fabric from her body. "I need…I must…gone." He was momentarily incapable of forming a complete sentence, but that was okay because Kira obviously felt the same way. Beneath him, she lifted her upper body up and shimmied the coat—and shirt beneath it—off and over her head, revealing a soft-pink lacy bra. The cups strained under the swell of her luscious breasts.

"Damn, girl."

Whatever blood was left in his body rushed straight to his cock, which strained at the crotch of his jeans. *Patience, Nash.* He tried to talk himself down, and think of anything besides her beautiful breasts that were heaving against the delicate lace that was so completely unexpected from the tough, independent Kira. The contrast was hot as hell.

"You are the most beautiful woman I've ever feasted my eyes on." He cupped his large hand over one perfect breast, squeezing and testing the weight of it. His thumb rubbed over her nipple until it stood, hard and hot, pressing through the lace. Nash lowered his mouth to the other breast, and pulled the nipple, lacy bra and all, between his lips. He sucked just hard enough to hear her moan, to make her back arch up off the ground. There was no doubt: if he reached into her jeans, he'd find her panties soaked with need for him.

But not yet.

His mouth worked relentlessly on first one nipple and then the other. She groaned when he used his teeth to bite just enough. He played with pressure, pushing her right to the edge of too much before he switched to a softer, almost delicate touch. Kira's groans intensified and she wriggled beneath him, craving release. Nash knew exactly how to get her to fall over the edge of passion, but selfishly, he was waiting to share that moment with her for the first time.

"Nash," Kira moaned and reached for him in an effort to pull him down. "I need you."

"I know you do, babe." With both hands, he squeezed her breasts together before he pressed a kiss between them. "But not as much as I need you." And then there was no more playing. With lightning-fast reflexes, Nash's hands moved to her jeans, tore down the zipper and tugged them over her hips and down to her ankles, where she kicked them off completely while Nash shed himself of his own jeans.

With nothing more between them, Nash settled himself between her creamy thighs and ran his hands up each one until his fingers reached the hot, wet apex.

With the slightest touch, Kira let out a noise and arched backward, pressing her hips up to meet him. "Nash...I...."

He swallowed her words with his mouth, kissing her hard as he slipped a finger into her wet heat. She gasped and tensed around him reflexively. *Damn. She was so sexy, so responsive to his touch, so completely perfect.*

She moaned for breath beneath him, and Nash knew if he let her up for breath, he'd be rewarded with the sexy sound of her passion, but that would be his undoing. He'd be totally unable to hold off from taking her and driving into her. And he wasn't ready. He still needed more.

He needed to give her everything. All that she could handle and then some more. Nash needed to take Kira right to the edge of shattering before pulling her back again. He needed to control her pleasure and play her body until he was finally good and ready to sink into her and crash into the orgasm with her.

Slowly at first, he moved one finger and then added another. He swallowed the sound of need with his kiss as he quickened the pace of his hand. Her body tightened around him and he knew she was close. He pulled his fingers away. Kira groaned her displeasure and reached for him.

She was growing impatient, but that was okay because as stubborn as she was, he was more so. "Patience, babe." He kissed her again. Slow and deep, it held the promise of everything that was yet to come and for the moment it placated her.

But it was only a moment, because Kira's hands ran down his stomach to his hips, his thighs, and then her hands were wrapped around his hard dick and Nash wasn't sure he'd ever felt anything so intense.

Kira stared him straight in the eyes. Even in the dim light, he could see the gleam of mischief all but overshadowed by thick passion. "When I know what I want, I only have so much patience, Nash. And I want you." She squeezed and stroked her hand up and down. A shudder of pleasure ripped through him. He was only barely holding on to his control. "And I want you now." She squeezed again, quickening her pace, and Nash knew he was lost.

Fuck it.

There'd be time to show her who was in control later. The time to satisfy the animal in both of them was now. "Jesus, babe." He closed his eyes for a moment, letting the magic of her touch soak in, and then he could no longer wait. A growl rose from his throat and his eyes were open. He stilled her hand, and used his strong thighs to push hers farther apart while he sat poised at her entrance.

She didn't have to say it; the want was in her eyes. With one thrust, slow at first, Nash entered her. Her heat enveloped him and the feeling was almost too much for him to handle. She felt better than he'd even imagined. *Perfect.*

He gave her a moment to grow accustomed to his size, but only a moment before he pushed farther, seating himself deep inside her.

Kira's head fell back, a moan of pleasure escaping her. All Nash wanted for their first time, was to ride the tide together.

As if she knew exactly what he was thinking, Kira wrapped her legs around him and drove her hips up to meet his. Her fingers dug into the muscles on his shoulders as they set a perfect pace. It wasn't long before Kira's body tightened around him. Nash was ready for it; his own orgasm was only barely restrained.

He quickened his pace and looked directly into her eyes, daring her to look away. She didn't.

At the exact moment she finally got her release, Nash felt his own climax spill forth. They each roared out in pleasure as they tumbled over the edge together.

His entire body vibrated with the aftershocks of his orgasm. At some point he must have closed his eyes or looked away, because Kira was no longer looking at him. Her eyes were shut tight, a small smile on her lips. Impulsively, Nash bent to kiss that smile. Her eyes still didn't open, but the smile got wider.

Satisfied, he rolled off her, lay next to her and pulled her into his embrace. One thing he knew for sure: whatever demons she was fighting when it came to him and whatever it was that was going on between them, for the first time since they'd met, his wolf was satiated.

And that was both deeply satisfying and intensely problematic.

For both of them.

CHAPTER SIX

Kira swore and her arm lashed out of the covers, ready to disarm the blaring alarm clock or hurl it across the room. Whatever came first. Her hand landed on the plastic and she smacked blindly until the blasting noise stopped. She groaned and rolled over, but it was too late. She wouldn't be going back to sleep.

Although she could easily have used another few hours of slumber, she'd already taken the later shift in the office, assigning Sasha and Conner to opening, which meant she would definitely owe Sasha a favor. She loved her friend, but Sasha wasn't known for her good mood in the mornings.

But she wasn't going to think about Sasha or Conner or anyone else. At least not for another few minutes.

Kira stretched her arms over her head and reveled in her deliciously sore muscles. It had been a long time since she'd been with a man, too long. But that didn't matter, not anymore. Because last night had made up for any dry spell she'd had.

More than made up for it.

She wanted to languish in bed all day, reliving the experience of the night before and how after, Nash had wrapped her in his arms and held him tight against his hard, hot body. Kira could still feel the weight of his arm draped over her, the way his hand lazily cupped her breast absentmindedly as he kissed the back of her neck and whispered stories of when he'd moved back to the park as a young teenager.

He told her about how he and his brother had spent their days running with the rest of the pack, giving the tourists a show. They'd been taught from the time they were small the importance of being a wolf and the meaning they had to Yellowstone and the rest of their kind. Listening to him speak with so much love and fondness laced through his voice, Kira couldn't help but remember her own youth, the time spent as a young cub with her brothers. She felt the flicker of pain knowing she wouldn't see them again, experience that free and easy time with them again. Instead of shutting down the pain, she let herself feel it. Let it sit inside her and burn a glowing ember.

Thinking of Axel, Luke, and especially her twin, Kade, usually caused pain that not so long ago had been unbearable. Last night, in Nash's arms, it had been different.

Not that it meant anything.

Nothing.

It meant nothing.

And she'd keep telling herself that, too. Because being with Nash had been amazing, but it wasn't a solution to the problems in her life and it definitely wasn't going to be anything more than what it was. He was a wolf. It could never be anything more than great sex.

Kira stretched one more time, her smile stretched across her face.

It had definitely been that.

But she couldn't lie in bed reliving it all morning. She had a job to do, so reluctantly Kira rolled out of bed and into the shower.

The hot water did nothing to erase the memory of Nash's hands on her body, however. She was still turned on twenty minutes later when she'd showered, dressed, and walked into the kitchen to pour herself her first cup of coffee.

"Good morning."

Kira's smile when she saw Nash, who certainly should have been at work hours ago, stretched her face tight. She was sure that every muscle in her face would be sore for days just from the constant smile of the last twenty-four hours.

"I didn't expect to see you here."

"I'm full of surprises." He handed her a cup of coffee, complete with a kiss on the cheek. "And quite honestly, I was a little worn-out after last night. Think the boss will mind?"

"Oh, I don't think so." She winked and laughed. "But I'm not really the boss."

"I'm fairly sure that if we called up management and told them about the mind-blowing sex we had last night while we were on stakeout to catch the fish culprits, they might have something to say about it. Especially since we didn't catch the fish culprits." Nash kissed the sensitive spot under her ear. "Are there even fish culprits? Maybe we should have done our job better?" His tongue traced a line to her ear.

"Oh, I think we did our jobs pretty damn well last night."

Nash laughed. "Maybe we should do it again tonight?"

"Maybe we should figure out what's killing the fish."

The mention of dead fish was the end of the kissing, and as much as Kira would have happily spent the rest of her day kissing Nash, the reminder of the dead fish plaguing her campground was a wakeup call to that fact. She slid away from his arms because the only way she was going to get any work done was by putting distance between them.

She took a sip of coffee. "I wonder if there are any new fish this morning? Maybe I should call Conner and find out what happened overnight."

"Or…" Nash opened the oven and produced a dish of something that smelled amazing. "Maybe it can wait a few more minutes and you can sit and have a nice breakfast with me? After all, there's a whole *morning after* procedure we should probably follow, don't you think?"

At the moment, Kira could think of a lot of things that they should probably be doing, but Nash's idea of a *morning after* procedure sounded pretty damn good to her. Plus, she was starving and whatever it was he'd prepared smelled amazing.

"Of course. Work can wait."

Kira quickly set the table and topped up each of their mugs while Nash dished them out each a plate. "Frittata." He presented the plate with a flourish and sat across from her.

She inhaled deeply, filling her senses with the aroma. "Thank you. You didn't have to do this."

Nash shrugged. "I wasn't kidding when I said we should do it again tonight, Kira." His smile did something to her insides. "Maybe without the stakeout part."

She laughed. "As much as I'd love to, I think we should probably figure out the mystery, don't you?"

He shrugged his consent. "Okay, but first, at least for this morning, can we talk about something besides dead fish? At least while we eat?"

"Of course." She took a bite of the egg dish and let it melt in her mouth. "There was something I wanted to ask you about."

"I'm all ears."

Kira bit back a sharp retort about canine hearing, and instead asked the question she'd been thinking about since the night before. "Last night you told me about your brother." He nodded. "I got the impression that you two are pretty close."

Nash shrugged one shoulder but didn't look at her. "We were once."

"And now?"

Kira knew she was pushing, but she really wanted to know.

"Now we're not." Nash attacked his frittata. "It happens with siblings. Didn't you say you had brothers?"

Surely, he was only trying to deflect from an uncomfortable question, but the question put her on the defense none the less. "I do." It was all she would normally be willing to say. "And like you, I guess we just aren't close anymore. It happens."

"It can." He shoved a bite in his mouth, chewed thoughtfully and asked, "Is that why you deny your bear?"

Kira almost choked on her coffee. "I...I don't..." She swallowed hard. "How did you know?"

"That you don't shift?"

Her shoulders sagged. Sadness and fatigue flooded through her, erasing her previous light mood. She nodded.

"Hey." Nash's voice was softer. "I wasn't trying to upset you."

"It's okay." And oddly, it was. Sure, thinking about her family, and the way she denied her true self, was hard, but it needed to be done. She couldn't avoid it. Not forever anyway. Besides, it was exhausting, holding it inside all the time. "You're right. I do deny my bear. I deny everything about myself and my past. It's easier that way."

"Easier?"

"It hurts less."

"Kira...talk to me." He put his fork down, crossed his hands in front of him on the table and stared into her eyes.

She sighed, letting the air leave her lungs before she looked up into his gray eyes. He was a wolf. She had no business telling him her secrets. From the time she was a cub, she'd been taught to stay away from wolves. It was family first, or not at all. And definitely not *dogs*. But he was watching her with real care and concern in his eyes. He wanted to know. She could see that. Besides, dog or not, not even twenty-four hours ago, he'd been inside her. And even if that had never happened, there was something about him. Despite herself, she felt closer to Nash than she'd felt with anyone. With the exception of her twin brother. But that was different. And it's not as if she'd be able to vent to Kade anytime soon.

What was the point of keeping it all in?

"Almost two years ago I made a choice that my family didn't agree with." She started talking. "I chose an unsuitable mate." Just thinking of Ryan and the word *mate* in the same sentence made her shudder now that she knew it was as far from the truth as she could get. "There was a group of young grizzlies traveling through my home territory and my grandfather forbade the females of our clan to go anywhere near them. Of course, I took that as a challenge."

Nash raised his brow. "Of course you did."

"Well, I fell for one of them." Nash's face twisted as he realized the direction her story was taking. "His name was Ryan Dixon and he was smooth, charming, and handsome."

"A deadly combination." Nash winked and for a moment, Kira smiled. And then she remembered.

"Ryan was also a liar, and a con. He convinced me that we were fated mates and meant to be together. He quickly wormed his way into my heart in a way I couldn't even begin to describe. The worst part was I believed everything he said. All of it. I fell for it." Remembering her naiveté stung, but it was part of the story, so she told it. "He said all the right things, telling me I was beautiful and sexy and how he couldn't stand to be apart from me for even a moment." She laughed, the sound harsh. "The craziest thing was we'd only known each other for a few days, so we didn't even have a chance to actually *be* apart. But I couldn't see that. I couldn't see anything except Ryan. He convinced me we were fated. *Fated.* And I fell for that. Do wolves have fated mates?"

It couldn't only be a bear thing, but she'd never thought to ask before. She'd never needed to know. But now, for reasons she didn't fully want to explore, it seemed very important.

"This is going to sound kind of stupid," Nash said. "But I don't really know if we do or not."

"How can you not know? Surely you know people who have fated mates? Or at least talk about it."

He shook his head and stared at her blankly. "I mean...maybe? Mates are chosen where I come from."

That was sad. To know that wolves would never feel the burning pull of a fated mate, it was just so...sad. But what was sadder? *Never being able to experience it? Or to be fooled into thinking you had it, just to be humiliated?* Kira's face burned hot with shame.

"Well, if wolves don't have fated mates, you're lucky. Because at least you'll never have to worry about what it's really supposed to feel like."

"What does that mean? What's it supposed to feel like? It seems that it would be a good thing."

"I wouldn't know," Kira said sadly. "I mean, I thought I did. I thought I had it with Ryan. But it was just lust and excitement and…make-believe. He made me believe it was true, but it wasn't. We weren't fated and by the time I realized it, it was too late."

If she was honest with herself, it was probably too late the moment she disobeyed her grandfather. Her brothers had known it, too. She was never the type of bear who was going to sit around and wait to be told what to do, and who to mate and how to live the rest of her life. She'd been yearning to go out on her own and experience life from the time she was a young cub. She'd never been cut out to lead the type of life her grandfather wanted for her.

Ryan had been an excuse. A reason to get out. And if she was really honest with herself, she knew that. She wanted to believe that they were fated mates because it made leaving that much easier. But even knowing why she'd fallen so easily, his betrayal still hurt because she *had* believed him.

"I let him convince me that our love was unstoppable," she continued. "Because that's what fated love is supposed to be. Unstoppable. No matter what obstacles are put between you and your mate, when you're fated, the instinct to be together is said to be so strong, it burns a fire inside you. Being apart is said to cause actual pain. The pull to be together, all-consuming."

"That doesn't sound very good."

"You don't think it's romantic?"

Nash laughed. "No. I think it sounds terrible." He reached for her hand and squeezed. "Tell me the rest."

Kira nodded and almost laughed herself because she couldn't disagree with him. It did sound terrible.

"There isn't a whole lot more to tell except I fell for it. I left with him and his clan mates. He told me we were headed to his clan's lands in Colorado but we only made it as far as the gate of Yellowstone before my brothers caught up with us."

"How many brothers do you have?"

"Three. Axel, Luke, and my twin, Kade." Her heart clenched just saying his name. "My grandfather sent them to bring me back."

"But you wouldn't go?"

She shook her head. "I was in love, remember? Fated." Saying it out loud made her want to spit. Or growl. "And because they love me, they believed me and accepted my choice. They left." Her heart caught in her throat. She swallowed down the pain, remembering the way they'd turned and walked away from her. At the time, Kira knew they were doing it out of love and respect for her, but it still hurt more than she'd ever thought was possible. "It was only a few days after they left that Ryan dumped me and the truth came to light. He'd used me to get back at my family. You see, the real reason my grandfather didn't want us to go anywhere near him and his clansmen was because our family had a long-standing feud with the Dixon clan. It dated back generations and my grandfather knew what I had to learn the hard way: nothing but trouble would come from that clan."

"So what happened? Why didn't you go home when you learned the truth?"

It was a question she'd only asked herself once, before she'd discovered the harsh reality that her twin brother had shunned her. "They didn't want me," she said simply. "I tried to reach out to Kade. Our bond as twins is stronger than a normal sibling bond. When we're in our bear forms, we can sense each other. Even from a distance. I'm told it's something like having a mate, but again, I wouldn't know." Her voice was devoid of the bitterness of her words. "Anyway, it was the first thing I did. As soon as I got the chance, I shifted and went for a run to call out for him. Nothing. So I did it again. Night after night after night, for months. But there was nothing. I couldn't even get a sense for him. He'd shut me off." The knot of pain that she'd carried with her deep in her stomach for years tightened. "It hurt more than the humiliation of Ryan's abandonment. A lot more. So that final night when I ran through the trees, reaching out for Kade, trying to connect with him, and got nothing, I made a decision."

"You'd deny your bear," Nash finished for her.

She nodded and reached for her coffee cup, cold now. "I didn't deserve it. And there was no point to it. They didn't want me. I needed to start over and that was easier if I wasn't a bear."

"But you are a bear."

Kira laughed. "Only if I want to be. It's worked up until now. Until you came along and sensed it."

"But I only barely sensed your bear."

"See? It's working."

Nash pushed back from his chair and came around the table. He pulled her into his strong arms and squeezed her tight before he pulled back, his hands firmly on her shoulders. "It is most definitely *not* working. You can't shut off who you are, Kira. I sensed your bear, even if it was hidden, because you *are* a bear and the longer you pretend you're not, the longer you're delaying your happiness. And Kira, even if you don't think you do, you deserve to be happy. You deserve everything and that starts with embracing your animal."

She shook her head and pulled out of his grip. She didn't want to look at him. The conversation had been too raw and far too real for first thing in the morning. Her glow from earlier had vanished and at that moment, she would have done anything to get it back. "I don't know if I can." Her voice was quiet and weak, almost defeated, and she hated it. "I'm afraid."

"Babe, you have nothing to be afraid of." Nash squeezed her arms and she looked up into his gray eyes. They were so full of kindness and an understanding she hadn't seen in anyone since…before…longer than she could remember. "That's what we're doing tonight," Nash declared.

"What?"

"We're going for a run." He smiled that toothy, sexy grin she was beginning to get very used to. "It's been far too long since I've let my animal out, and while I thought last night would have gone a long way in satisfying him…well, I was wrong."

There was a lot in that statement Kira wanted to address, but it would have to wait because there were more pressing issues. "I can't," she said. "It's been too long."

Nash chuckled. "Admittedly, I don't know a ton about bears," he said. "But I can't imagine that part of things is too terribly different from wolves. It's not like it's use-it-or-lose-it situation, Kira. You'll be able to shift."

"But…what if…." She trailed off because she couldn't think of a good excuse. In fact, she was fairly positive that there was no such thing as an excuse good enough to satisfy Nash when it came to this. He was like a dog with a bone. The comparison made her laugh inappropriately, and he took the moment to pounce.

"Come on, Kira. And you know what they say…sex is always better after a good run."

For the first time in forever, Kira found herself actually entertaining the idea. And then, with the weight of Nash's hands on her shoulders, his musky scent filling her senses, and his eyes boring into hers, she said, "Okay."

CHAPTER SEVEN

The day had taken forever to go by. But not because Nash had a lack of work to do. In fact, now that the camping season was starting to pick up, his workload had only increased. There were campsite signs to fix from the inevitable trailers that backed into them, more picnic tables to repair, a seemingly unending amount of clogged toilets, and never mind the actual maintenance work he had from the head office.

No, time hadn't moved slowly because he was bored. All Nash could think about all day was what was going to happen later that night. Getting Kira alone the first time had been nothing short of amazing. Getting her alone the second time would be absolutely mind-blowing. Because as soon as he was able to sneak her away from the cabin, they were going to go out into the woods and shift.

Just thinking about how good it would feel to stretch his muscles and run with Kira by his side fueled the raging erection he'd had almost all day. Not only was he going to have the chance to see Kira in her true form, he'd be the one to help her return to her animal self. He couldn't imagine the pain and hurt it must have cost her to go without shifting for so long.

But all that would change. Tonight.

Nash pulled into his parking spot at the staff cabin and cut the engine. He had just enough time for a shower and change before they were set to leave. Kira had said something about leaving early so they could have a picnic before it got dark. It sounded an awful lot like a date to Nash, and to his surprise, he had absolutely no problem with that. There were a million reasons he *should* have a problem with it, or be scared, even a little. But he didn't. Not at all.

His brother, on the other hand...Nolan would very much have a problem if he heard Nash was going on a *date* with a bear. Would he ever.

But Nash didn't want to think about Nolan, or anyone else for that matter. No one mattered but him and Kira and what they were going to do later that night. Because however it turned out, one thing was for sure: it was going to be good.

He slammed the door of the truck behind him and was headed up to the cabin when he got intercepted. "You look happy. Must have been a good day plunging toilets."

Nash narrowed his eyes at the man who'd come up beside him. But only for a minute. He wasn't worth the energy. "Conner," he said by way of greeting. Nash had only had the opportunity, if you could call it that, to sit down and talk to the man a few times, but that was all he needed to formulate his opinion. Conner was a bitter, angry guy. Why, Nash had no idea, but as long as he didn't have to spend much time with him and his toxic attitude, Nash couldn't care less. "My day was great. Thanks for asking."

"Mine sucked."

"I didn't ask." Nash flashed him a smile that he was certain would just piss Conner off. "You should really try harder to have more positive working days, Conner. Life is too short to be stuck in a job you hate, don't you think?"

He reached for the door a step before Conner got there, and held it open for the other man, who only looked more irritated by the gesture.

Nash shook his head with a smile. There really was no pleasing the guy.

"Whatever," Conner muttered under his breath. "You'd probably have a shitty day, too, if you had guests complaining about the stink of rotting fish next to their campsite."

Nash stopped short. He hadn't even thought to ask about the fish problem that morning and despite the fact that they were supposed to have been on a stakeout the night before to see what was causing it, he hadn't given the problem any thought at all. "There were more fish this morning? I didn't hear anything."

"Yeah, there were fish." Conner went to the shared fridge and took a beer without offering Nash one. "And these ones were rotted and disgusting. They weren't in the same spot either. Farther downstream, in a pile by site 36." He cracked the top of his can and swallowed deep. "And they weren't happy about it, either. Have you ever had to deal with a pissed-off guest, Nash? It sucks because all you can do is smile and nod like an idiot and promise you'll look into the problem. You're pretty much a pussy with a—"

"I'd appreciate if you didn't use that kind of language in here, Conner." Kira walked into the kitchen. Nash's dick twitched at the sight of her. "After all," Kira continued as she walked across the room toward Nash, "it's not very respectful toward women, and we all live here."

Conner muttered something under his breath, took another swig of his beer and glared at Kira, who'd come to

70

stand by Nash. "Maybe if you figured out why the fish were dying, I wouldn't have to deal with the problem at all and we wouldn't have pissed-off guests who were pulling up and heading to different campgrounds."

"They're leaving?" Kira's voice was laced with concern.

"Of course they're leaving," Conner spat. "Why would they stay in a campground that stunk, and was being managed by a woman who was more interested in sneaking off with the maintenance man than running a quality campground where they can spend their family holiday?"

"Okay, that's enough." Nash stepped forward, slightly in front of Kira. He had no doubt that she could take care of herself, none at all, but that wasn't the point. The point was that this asshole was disrespecting his mate and he wasn't going to stand for it.

Mate?

Nash froze, only mildly aware that Conner had stepped up to him.

Holy fuck. Mate?

Where had that come from? He couldn't go around thinking of Kira as a mate. There were so many reasons that was wrong and never going to happen.

But there were also a lot of reasons it was so very right.

Nash shook his head and focused on the little man who'd stepped up, fists clenched, very much in Nash's personal space. He didn't have time for any disruptive thoughts about Kira. He also didn't have time for Conner, who was clearly itching for a fight.

"Back off, little man." Nash kept his voice light and stepped past him to the fridge to get a beer of his own. Not because he wanted one, but he needed something to cool him down and think of anything but what had just happened. Even if it was in his head.

"Want one?" Nash turned to look at Kira with a beer in

his hand.

She looked at him strangely, but after a moment shook her head. "No. Thanks." She turned to Conner. "You need to check yourself, Conner. We may be off the clock, but I'm still your boss."

Conner glanced between them, his eyes narrowed in a glare. For a second, Nash thought the man was going to challenge him again, but then he took a step back and swallowed hard. "Okay," he said. It definitely wasn't an apology, but Kira didn't look like she was going to press it. "But take care of the fish thing," Conner added. "Or I'm going to have to tell the head office. I'm sick of dealing with angry guests who think the water is poisoned."

He stomped off like a teenager having a tantrum. Nash half expected to hear a door slam. Not that he cared, but it was good to have him gone. He really didn't need to risk getting into a fistfight and losing his job. Especially not over a guy as weaselly as Conner.

Besides, he had way more important things to think of. Like getting Kira out of there and out to the woods, where they could be alone.

Kira would be lying if she said she wasn't nervous about shifting. The truth was that she was terrified.

Not of the actual shifting part. That she was looking forward to. The way her body would stretch and relax all at the same time. The feeling of nothing between her and the fresh air. The rustle of the wind in her fur. All of it. Never mind the way her mind would relax. All of the pent-up emotion and energy she'd been stuffing down for the last year would melt away. Sex with Nash had helped, but nothing was quite like shifting into her bear to give herself a reset.

Yes, she was definitely looking forward to the shifting part. That wasn't the problem.

The part that she'd been worrying about and stressing over all day was far more complicated.

Distracting herself with work all day hadn't worked, and she'd hoped that when she finally got to see Nash, that just being with him would put her worries at ease. But they'd only increased as she got into the truck next to him and drove to the picnic spot Kira had chosen.

She'd hardly paid any attention on the drive, and it wasn't until she led him down a trail past a thermal hot spot that would lead to the perfect picnic spot that she had in mind, that Nash finally called her on her distraction.

"What's going on, Kira? You seem like you're a million miles away today."

She forced a smile that she was sure he'd see right through and kept walking. "I was just trying to remember exactly how to get to my spot." She was a terrible liar. A fact he pointed out a moment later.

"You're full of shit." Nash chuckled. "But I know it's been awhile since you've shifted, so I won't push. I get it. If you want to talk about it, I'm here."

Kira exhaled long and hard. Of course he got it. Nash understood her in a way she'd never experienced before. He just had a sense about her and what she needed, what she was thinking and...well, everything. Being with him was easy and awesome and just got more so the longer they spent together. When she thought about how hard she'd tried to resist him, she could hardly believe it had been less than a month.

So much had changed.

And it was about to change even further.

"So, where are we going?"

She was grateful for the subject change. "It's this great

little spot I discovered. The park hasn't made a trail up here yet, so only people who know to look for it will find it. And at this time of year, we should have it to ourselves."

"And what is it?"

"You'll see." She winked at him and continued along the trail that was so faint, she wouldn't have even known it was there if it weren't for her bear instincts. Muted as they were, they still helped with anything involving the outdoors.

Another few minutes of walking and they arrived at their destination, an opening in the trees, at the top of a cliff that overlooked the river and a set of bubbling pools of thermal waters, some of which were spouting little geysers. Kira set down her backpack, put her hands on her hips and breathed in a lungful of fresh air, laced with just the slightest bit of sulfur from the thermals below. She surveyed the land around them, and just as she'd expected, they were all alone. "Isn't it incredible up here?"

Nash wrapped his arms around her from behind and kissed her neck. "You're pretty incredible."

Kira leaned back and sank into him. Everything between them had happened so quickly, but it didn't matter because the ease between them felt comfortable and familiar while at the same time exciting the hell out of her. With his arms still around her, Kira pointed to the pools of thermals below them. "Watch," she said. "We're just in time."

"Time for what?"

"The geyser is going to erupt. This is the best seat in the house. The best part is not many people even know about this thermal pool because it's not easily accessible and almost no one knows about this spot. It'll be like a private show."

They spread out a blanket and Kira pulled out the picnic

before she sat down next to Nash. "How do you know when it's going to erupt?" he asked. "Is it like Old Faithful?"

"Yes and no. It erupts fairly regularly, but not as frequently as the big famous one. This one only goes off every week or so."

"Ahh. And being that it's so far off the road, probably not worth developing into a major tourist site. Gotcha." Nash picked up one of the sandwiches she'd prepared. "I would say that I'm surprised I'd never heard of it, but I grew up on the other side of the park and our pack didn't roam around very much."

She watched him eat for a moment before she asked the question she'd been dying to know the answer to. "So why did you leave? I mean, you told me a little bit about your brother, but—"

The geyser beneath them erupted in a huge spout of water that shot up past their vantage point in a roar, interrupting Kira's question. Nash slipped his arm around her and squeezed. "That's pretty amazing," he said. "It doesn't matter how many times you see it. It truly is a phenomenon."

She nodded in agreement, her question forgotten for the moment as they watched the show. The water fell and rose, multiple times until finally it splashed to the ground as if someone had suddenly cut off the water supply and just like that, it was over.

"That was incredible."

"*You're* incredible." Nash turned her easily in his arms and kissed her. His hand cupped her face and held her to him as their tongues clashed together. It only took seconds before he had her entire body on fire. The need she had for him was almost explosive and it threatened to completely consume her every time they touched.

Nash pulled away, ending the kiss. "Are you ready?"

"For what?" All Kira could think about was his mouth on her skin, her hands clawing down his back while he pressed inside her, but the look in his eyes alerted her to something else. "Oh. That." Her desire faded away, replaced again by apprehension. "But it's still daylight."

"You said yourself that we are all alone up here and I think it'll be good for you to run in the light." He stood and offered her a hand up. "Besides, I want to see you without the shade of night."

Kira's body trembled and she swallowed hard. "Okay," she said before she could change her mind. She took his hand and he pulled her to her feet easily before immediately leading her away from the ledge and toward the protection of the trees.

They didn't speak while they stripped their clothes off. Kira folded hers into a neat stack; Nash tossed his into a pile next to hers and then they were naked. Any other time, she would have relished the fact that Nash and his lean, muscular, completely perfect body stood only a few feet away from her own nakedness. But she was too focused on what was about to happen.

You can do this, Kira. Just shut off your thoughts. Right. She could do that. She could shift and not think about her brothers or home or anything. *Why not? Of course she could do that.* She'd just focus on the feeling of being in her bear and running through the woods. And Nash. She could focus on the wolf. She'd never run with a wolf before. Not even close.

Kira nodded and smile to herself, feeling dramatically better. "Why didn't I think of that before?" she muttered to herself, feeling foolish for her earlier nerves.

Nash gave her a sidelong glance but thankfully didn't press her. He knew she was preoccupied with a host of

Elena Aitken

different thoughts. "Ready?"

She nodded.

His mouth slipped into his super sexy signature smile. A flash of desire ripped through her the way it always did, but she didn't have time to process it because a second later, Nash leapt into the air.

The transformation was dramatic and beautiful as his long, lean body stretched forward into the air. The most magnificent wolf Kira had ever seen hit the ground. He took a few steps upon landing. His black fur, streaked with silver and gray, shimmered in the sun and Kira was thankful for the daylight so she could admire it. She stood for a moment, dumbfounded at the beauty in front of her before his large head swung around. Nash's familiar gray eyes watched her.

Nash twitched his head, beckoning her. He took a few more steps and turned to wait. And watch.

A shiver ripped through her. Kira closed her eyes, swallowed hard and started to run.

Watching Kira shift into her true form was the sexiest thing Nash had ever seen. She was magnificent in her bear. A beautiful, dark grizzly, she looked incredibly fierce when she hit the ground running.

And she was running. Into the trees and away from him.

Nash chuckled and shook his heavy head before he pursued her.

The shift would be a difficult one for Kira, especially considering it had been so long since the last time she was in her animal form. It would be exhausting and there was no telling how long she'd be able to stay in her bear. Nash wasn't positive that it was the same as it was for him, but it had to be similar. Shifting was like a muscle. The more you used it, the easier it got. And likewise, if you went too long denying your true self, it took awhile to build up your stamina again.

That being said, Kira didn't seem to have any trouble at the moment. She was moving quickly, but Nash was strong, too, and caught up with her seconds later.

How does it feel?

As if in response, Kira tipped back her head and let out a mighty roar that shook the earth, before she slowed her pace. Nash slowed with her, and howled his happiness in return because it felt damned good to feel his muscles stretch and pull. But mostly it felt amazing to be side by side with Kira who, after way too long, was embracing her true self. That felt friggin' fantastic.

Their pace slowed, and finally stopped as they made their way into a clearing where a family of deer enjoyed an evening meal. Their ears flicked toward the two predators, and a flash later they were gone.

Kira sat hard on her haunches and started to laugh. Nash looked from her to where the deer had taken off and, realizing what she was likely laughing at, joined in. There was no doubt that for the deer, seeing a wolf and grizzly together must look like a nightmare come to life.

The laughter quickly faded as he was struck once again by how majestic she was.

He dipped his head and looked away, overwhelmed with feelings he'd never felt before.

Nash.

He'd heard her say his name. But not with her voice. It was different. He'd never been able to communicate in his wolf form before.

Ever.

It was only hearing his name that Nash realized she'd heard him earlier too when he'd wondered how she felt while running.

Damn. What was happening?

He lifted his head and looked into her deep eyes, widened with as much surprise and wonderment as he felt.

Kira.

He had to know, even though he couldn't properly express what *it* was.

Slowly, she got to her feet.

Kira walked toward him, so her snout was only inches from his. Everything about the situation was wrong. A wolf and a bear didn't...they couldn't...but they did. That was the part that was so crazy to him. The laws of nature, and more importantly of their clans, said they weren't supposed to be together. They were breaking all the rules. But it didn't matter. Not even a little. Now that they were each in their true forms, everything was becoming very clear.

Whatever it was that was happening, even if he could put it into words, Nash wouldn't have to explain anything because it was *everything* and if she felt it, she'd know.

If she was honest with herself, he knew what she'd say.

Finally, after what felt like forever, Kira nodded.

It scared the hell out of him, because as far as Nash knew, no one in his pack had ever had the experience of finding their true mate. The one that their body yearned for, that they were connected to in a primal way, the one that completed them. *Fated.* But that's exactly what he was feeling. And Kira felt it too. The knowledge of that propelled him forward, needing to be closer to her.

He nuzzled into her, inhaling her scent. He needed to be close with her, touching her, because he was terrified that if he wasn't, whatever was going on with them would disappear and all at once, he wasn't sure he could survive that.

CHAPTER EIGHT

For the next few weeks, the stress of the start of the season started to slip away. Kira fell into her groove as campsite manager, and even Conner stopped giving her such a hard time. The guests started coming in droves and everyone was busier than ever. But even amid their busy schedules, Kira and Nash found time to spend together. A lot of time.

Something had happened after the first time they shifted together. Kira had concentrated so completely on not trying to reach out to her brother, or utilize any form of twin connection, that she hadn't thought about any of the other things that could happen when she was in her bear form.

Not that she ever would have considered the idea that she would have such an intense experience with Nash. It was so different than how things were with Kade. As twins, they could sort of *feel* the other and experience generalized feelings. But with Nash, it was different. It was more acute, more tangible if that was even possible. When Nash's voice popped into her head as if he was speaking the words himself, she damn near fell over. The craziest part was that instead of freaking her out, it felt perfectly natural. As though she was always meant to be connected with Nash.

And that's what it was. A connection. Like a strand of thread joining them together. It was both terrifying and incredibly natural all at the same time. Nash felt it too and although they never talked about what had happened, it was as if they'd both come to a mutual agreement that whatever had happened—or more accurately, *was* happening between them—was exactly what should be.

Every few nights after that, they made a point to sneak off and go for a run. Usually under the pretense of investigating the ongoing mystery of the dead fish even though the truth was, they were too preoccupied with each other to focus on that specific situation. Which had to change, and soon.

Conner had warned her on more than one occasion that he would go to the head office if he had to deal with any more guest complaints, and she had no doubt he'd make good on the threat, which was why Kira had an entirely new plan to catch the culprit who was planting the fish. Because it had to be intentional. There was no other explanation; there were no reports of dead fish anywhere else in the park, so natural causes could be ruled out.

No, it was definitely a person. And tonight she was going to find out who it was. Which was why she hadn't told anyone what she was doing. Not even Nash. Although she had a feeling he'd figure it out pretty quickly.

Kira and her cabin mates had a rare dinner together earlier in the evening and even rarer, everyone was in a good mood. Even Conner. The whole group was settling in to play a card game and as much as she would have liked to stay and play, Kira faked a sore stomach and begged off. They'd long since given up trying to hide their relationship, so when Nash tried to insist on laying down with her, Kira made a big production of not wanting him to see her with the flu, and she'd more or less slammed the door in his face. She felt bad about lying to him, but she needed everyone to think she was alone in bed.

She'd waited until the house got quiet and the light that came from under her door, went out. Nash had knocked at one point to check on her, but she sent him away with a story about how she'd been vomiting. Finally, after what felt like forever, she stripped her clothes off and snuck out her window, where she shifted quickly into her bear.

It was risky to shift so close to humans. *Very* risky, but it was important.

She wasn't about to hang around, though. She took off for the cover of the trees at a blistering pace and made her way across the river, where she could lay down and watch for anything suspicious.

Over the last few weeks, since the very first stakeout that Kira and Nash went on, there had been a handful of more real attempts. Sometimes Sasha joined her, but mostly Nash was her partner. Every time someone went out watching, the dead fish didn't show up the next day, or like after the first time, they were discovered in a big, stinky pile somewhere else, as if the culprit dumped them when they couldn't fulfill their task. Obviously, Kira's theory was that knowing he—or she—was being watched, the fish bandit got spooked when they saw people and fled. By shifting into her bear, she was hoping she'd blend in with the surroundings a little better. She'd kept her plan quiet in case the culprit was among them, not even telling Nash. Not that she thought Nash was involved, but she didn't want to arouse suspicion in anyone, and it was better if she just kept quiet completely. She definitely had a few ideas who might be behind the problem, but she couldn't say anything unless she had hard proof.

Which was why she was about to settle in for the night,

camouflaged as a slumbering bear.

It was almost funny to Kira how quickly she'd embraced her bear again. There was no doubt in her mind that being with Nash had a lot to do with it.

Being with Nash.

It was still so crazy to think about it that way, but that's how it was. She was *with* Nash. A wolf.

She found a tree that would act as good cover and settled down into the earth, her mind still preoccupied with the wolf who had occupied pretty much every waking thought, and sleeping ones too, since they'd met.

The whole thing was so wrong. After all, a bear and a wolf, together? It was unthinkable. It went against everything she'd ever been taught. But the longer Kira spent on her own, away from the thoughts and ideals of her family and clan, the more she realized that maybe her grandfather didn't know everything about how things were *supposed* to be. As each day went by and she and Nash spent more and more time getting to know each other, Kira's heart only felt more full. And wasn't *that* the way things were supposed to be?

Besides, it wasn't as if she was involved with her family anymore anyway.

The thought no longer filled her with sadness the way it had only a few short months ago. She didn't even have to wonder why that was. Kira no longer felt alone because every fiber in her body thrilled when Nash was around—hell, even if he wasn't around. She only had to think of him for her body to explode. It was so different from the way things had felt with Ryan. That had just been a mistake.

A colossal mistake.

The night darkened around her; the sounds of the forest changed as the night grew longer. Kira settled her head onto her paws. But she didn't sleep. Shifting and maintaining her bear form had become much easier, just as it had become much easier not to think about her brother or to reach out using her twin bond when she was in bear form. The first few times, she'd had to concentrate on not thinking about Kade, until it became almost second nature to ignore the urge to try to connect. *Almost.*

Maybe it was that she was by herself. Or maybe it was that Kira was no longer desperate to connect with Kade. Whatever it was, as she laid under the tree and scanned the riverbank on the other side for signs of any strange activity, a thought began to take shape.

It probably wouldn't hurt. Even if there's no change, it won't matter.

Before she could change her mind or talk herself out of it, Kira closed her eyes and pictured her brother. She didn't expect anything to happen. Not really. And at first, nothing did. She couldn't sense him. She could barely remember what he looked like, what he sounded like, what his hug felt like.

And then it happened.

His face. His laugh. His back as he walked away.

The visions smashed through her so hard and so unexpectedly, they took her breath away. She felt as if she were rolling and tumbling down a hill from the force of the sensation. But when she opened her eyes again, she found she hadn't moved from her spot under the tree.

But it was so real.

Kira's breath came in pants. She tucked her big head under her arms and forced her breathing to slow. And then it happened.

Kira.

She snapped her head up and scanned her surroundings.

Nothing.

Kira?

It had to be Kade. Or was it Nash reaching out? He might be concerned about her. *What if he'd gone to check on her and she wasn't in her room?* That had to be it. The fact that she could connect with Nash in her bear form had surprised her, certainly, but over the last few weeks, she'd grown used to it. She'd looked forward to it. Connecting with Nash made her feel safe, secure…loved. She couldn't quite pinpoint her feelings for him, but it was unlike anything she'd ever felt before. That much she knew for certain. And she never wanted it to end.

Kira?

The call of her name hit her again, pulling her from her thoughts. It wasn't Nash calling her.

It was different. Yet familiar at the same time.

Was she really so tired that she couldn't distinguish between what it felt like to sense her own twin brother and the wolf she was sleeping with?

The entire thought was ludicrous.

She stood and stretched. She was tired. She was starting to mix up all her feelings, that's all. She never should have tried to reach out to Kade when she was so tired and feeling so run-down. Besides, she had way too much on her mind to think straight. Nash was probably looking for her and it was time to go.

That's all it was.

And that's exactly what she kept telling herself, the stakeout forgotten, until she got back to the cabin and slipped back through the window into her room. She kept telling herself that until she crossed the hall, opened Nash's door, and slid into bed next to him, where, just as she expected, he was waiting for her.

"Hey." Nash lifted his arm and Kira scooted in close until she was tucked in tight. "Are you feeling better? I was worried about you."

She tipped her head up to his, and even in the dim light of the moonlit room, he could see the question in her eyes. "You knew I wasn't sick?"

He nodded and kissed the top of her head. "I knew you needed some time alone. Besides, do you think that if I really thought you were sick I wouldn't even bother checking on you? Come on, babe. You should know better than that."

"What should I know?" Her voice was laced with mischief.

Her hand stroked his bare chest. Nash let out a little moan, because her hot touch on his skin never failed to stir him. Especially when her hand started to slide down his torso the way it was currently doing.

There was no doubt what she had on her mind, and of course Nash always had the same thing on his mind, too. But there were a few things he needed to say to her first. "You should know exactly how I feel about you, Kira." He placed a hand on hers, stilling its travel south. "And I hope you know exactly what that means for me." Nash let the silence go for a few minutes before he asked, "You do know, right?"

She stilled beneath him but then answered, "I think so. I'm just not entirely sure I know what it means."

It meant everything. He just didn't know how to tell her that. He'd been wrestling with what he was feeling, unsure of how exactly to tell Kira what he was thinking and feeling. He'd been waiting for the right time, but there never seemed to be a *right* time. Because he was terrified he'd scare her away.

Nash wrapped his arm tighter around her. "I don't have a lot of experience with things like this, Kira." He swallowed hard and continued. "I already told you that in my pack, mates aren't a choice you make—they're chosen for you. So quite honestly, I don't even know if how I'm feeling is normal or not, or even if there is any normal anymore. But all I know is—"

"Did you say *mate*?"

He squeezed her arm and twisted so she was underneath him. He hovered over her, able to look down in her dark, sexy eyes when he said what he needed to say. "I did." He waited for that to sink in. "And like I said, I don't even really know what it means right now, but I..." Her eyes had filled with unshed tears. "I'm sorry," he added quickly. "I wasn't trying to upset you or scare you or...well, the very last thing I wanted to do was make this—"

"You didn't." Kira's hand came up to his face and cupped his cheek. Her fingers scratched the scruff of a beard that had started there. "I'm not scared," she clarified. "The exact opposite, in fact."

"Yeah?"

She nodded and smiled and it was the sexiest thing he'd ever seen. "Yeah. In fact..." Kira wiggled until her other arm was free from the blankets and she wrapped them both around his neck. "I feel the same way."

Of course she did. He already knew without a doubt that she felt exactly the same way he did and it was long past time he did something about it.

A deep growl rumbled within him. Nash knew his animal would not be satisfied until he made her his. And that's exactly what he was going to do.

He kissed her hard and thoroughly. It was a kiss of possession and desire and when he pulled back, she was gasping, her face flushed with need. Her hands dropped away from his neck, and Nash seized the opportunity to shift and grab both her wrists with one large hand and pinned her arms above her head. Kira's eyes widened with surprise.

And desire.

He let his eyes move slowly over her body. Every curve, every dip, every sexy inch of her. Then, with his free hand, he traced a finger slowly down her neck. Kira moaned and turned her head, giving him greater access. He followed his finger with his tongue, licking and tasting the smooth, sensitive skin down to the swell of her breast.

Nash took one breast in his hand, letting his thumb flick over her nipple before he pinched it between two fingers. Kira made a sexy sound that had his cock throbbing, but he wasn't ready yet. With his hand occupied with her nipple, he sucked the other one between his lips where he bit down, just a little.

She screamed out her pleasure, and it was almost Nash's undoing.

With more restraint, he did it again, and again, until she writhed beneath him.

"You like that." It wasn't a question, but her eyes, hooded with desire and need, were all the answer he needed.

Once more, Nash slid up her body, his hand still holding her arms firmly in place over her head. He took his time, savoring the heat in her body, the way her breasts heaved beneath him, her hips pressed up into him, desperate for more. And she'd get it. He'd give her everything. Always. But first, he had to claim her. He needed to quench the fire raging through his veins. It was time.

"Kira." His voice was rough. "I need you. Forever."

She nodded, understanding in her eyes.

He could smell her desire, her need. He knew instinctually she was ready for him. And although he'd like nothing more than taking his slow, sweet time with her, that would come later. Now, he needed to make her his.

Leaving her hands clasped over her head, Nash shifted until he was poised at her entrance. Kira's eyes clouded with passion and she moved beneath him, pulling against his grip. He knew she wanted to be in control; she craved it because she was the finest damn alpha female he'd ever seen. Which was exactly what made her the perfect match for him, and he'd let her have her control. But not today. This was his.

His cock throbbed against her wet heat and Kira groaned.

He lifted his hips and with a smooth, hard thrust was inside her. Kira's sweet, hot heat enveloped him. Nash gave himself a moment to savor the feeling of his cock inside her, but then he was moving.

Together, they found their rhythm immediately. Nash's free hand slipped between them and found Kira's clit. He pressed down with just enough pressure and she groaned. She was close, but it had to be together.

"Babe, you are the sexiest fucking woman I—"

"Kiss me," she demanded. Control or not, Nash was not one to deny a request. His mouth crashed to hers; their tongues immediately entwined, thrusting into each other's mouths, battling for dominance. Her need to try to control was the sexiest thing he'd ever experienced, but today, need or not, she was his.

She protested with a groan when he pulled his mouth from hers. He responded by thrusting into her harder than before and her eyes closed to absorb the sensation. He could feel her body begin to tense. He was close, too.

"Open your eyes." It was his turn to make demands. She did as requested. "You're mine, Kira." He thrust again. "My love." And again, their climaxes were right on the edge. "My mate." With one final thrust, Nash barred his teeth and bit into the underside of her arm, still held over her head, as their mutual orgasms crashed through them.

Kira screamed out with the pleasure and pain of their mating.

When his powerful climax was finally spent, Nash pulled back and examined his mark. He dropped tender kisses around the bite, soothing her.

Perfect.
Beautiful.
His.

CHAPTER NINE

"I still can't believe you bit my arm."

Kira gingerly slid her arm into her uniform, trying her best to avoid the bite mark. Shifters healed quickly, but the bite mark Nash had left was not disappearing as fast as she would have expected.

"Babe, I didn't *bite* you. I *claimed* you." Nash came up behind her and wrapped his arms around her waist. "Big difference." He pushed her hair aside and kissed the back of her neck, sending a fresh thrill through her. "Besides, it had to be your arm."

She turned in his arms. "Why did it have to be my arm? People will see it there."

"Only if they're looking." Nash slid his fingers along her skin, until they traced his bite mark. "And it's not like a regular wound. It won't go away completely. It will leave a beautiful silver scar."

A scar? The idea gave her an unexpected thrill.

"And besides, the mark isn't for them, babe. It's for us."

"Us?"

He grinned. "Absolutely. Every time you feel the outline of my mark, or your tender skin rubbing against your clothes, you're going to remember me inside you, making you scream out." Kira's body vibrated with the need she always seemed to be right on the edge of when Nash was around. "And every time I catch a glimpse of my mark, I'm going to remember the way you looked under me, your naked body hot and ready and begging for me to make you mine."

A pool of moisture gathered between her legs, and if she wasn't already running late, Kira would have been more than happy for Nash to make her his over and over again. But she had to get dressed and get into the registration office. She'd already pushed it too far. Nash's hands slid down her body, over her hips and... *Maybe she could be a few more minutes?*

No.

She shook her head and forced herself to move out of Nash's grip. He was like a drug. And she was happily addicted.

"I have to get to work." Kira used her firmest voice, more to convince herself than Nash. She tugged her pants on and tucked her shirt in before she fastened her belt. "You will have to wait until later."

"Baby, I'll wait forever for you if I have to."

She kissed him chastely on the lips. "I won't make you wait that long." Before she could step back, Nash pulled her close and kissed her properly until a fresh wave of desire washed through her.

Damn. Distance was going to be the only thing that helped her move on with her day. Their passion had only grown stronger since he'd claimed her.

Claimed her. It was still crazy to think about. She wouldn't have thought it was possible to mate a bear with a wolf. But when it came down to it, nothing had felt more right—and crazy or not, that was the only thing that mattered.

"Okay, I really have to go." She pulled away before she could get sucked in for another kiss. "Shouldn't you get to work, too?"

Nash waved his hand, dismissing her comment. "How can I work after the most amazing night of my life?"

She knew he was teasing, but there was so much truth in his words that Kira couldn't help but smile. "Seriously." She tried to sound stern. "You should get to work."

"I will, I will." Nash reached out and grabbed her arm. "Before you go, I really just wanted to ask you something." His face shifted so quickly, worry pricked at her spine. His teasing smile was gone, replaced by a mask of seriousness.

"What is it?"

He slowly pulled her close, but didn't kiss her this time. "I just wanted to make sure you were okay. With everything that happened last night, I mean."

"I...of course...I..." Words escaped her. But that was crazy, because of course she was okay with everything. *Wasn't she?*

Nash reached out and stroked a strand of her hair, not yet tied back in her signature braid. "Because I know it was a lot," he said. "What happened between us. I know it might feel a little..."

"Crazy?"

He smiled. "I was going to say intense."

Kira nodded. That was a good word choice, too.

"But as crazy or intense as it all was," Nash continued, "it was right, too. Don't you think?" When she didn't answer right away, he added, "Me and you? *We're* right."

She nodded again. But this time found her words. "Yes. We are right. I feel it, Nash. I always have. I think that's why I resisted you so much when I first met you. It was all too *intense*," she said, using his word. "And I'm not going to pretend how it makes sense," she continued. "A wolf and a bear? It's…well, I guess it just is."

He kissed the tip of her nose. "It is." His strong arms wrapped around her into the warmest, most secure hug Kira had ever experienced and in that moment, she knew: *crazy, intense, weird,* or whatever other word anyone could come up with, it didn't matter because all that really mattered was that together, they were *right. Mates.*

One more kiss and Kira finally managed to slip out of Nash's bedroom and make her way into work. She'd been bracing herself for a phone call about more dead fish, but it never came and she really hoped it wouldn't. After all, she hadn't seen anything the night before and if there were no dead fish discovered today, that would be two days in a row that everything was good. Definitely a trend, no matter how small, in the right direction. Maybe whoever was responsible for the mess—and it was definitely a someone, of that much Kira was sure—had grown tired of their game and moved on?

Yes.

That was the attitude Kira would take. The perpetrator had moved on and everything would be fine from now on. She almost laughed aloud at her rose-colored attitude, but everything seemed a little brighter after last night with Nash, so why shouldn't it carry through all aspects of her life?

"There you are." Sasha's voice burst through her thoughts. Kira turned to see her friend in the doorway of the registration office. "Where've you been?" She wiggled her eyebrows, but Kira was not about to give her any details. Especially after what had really happened the night before. She was not one to kiss and tell, and she was most certainly not one to *bite*—or have been bitten—and tell.

94

"Sorry," Kira said. "I slept in a little."

"Are you feeling better?"

It took her a moment to remember her lie from the day before, but then it came back to her and she nodded. "Much. Thanks for asking."

"Good." Sasha stepped out of the building and closed the door, looking behind her. "Because someone is here to see you."

Kira's heart leapt into her throat. *Damn it. If the campground general manager had found out about the dead fish problem...* Maybe someone had reported it and she was going to catch shit for not reporting it, or worse, maybe she would lose her job. She couldn't lose her job, not now that she'd found Nash and together they were going to have the perfect summer. If she had to move, it would mean—

"Kira!"

She blinked once, twice.

Sasha waved a hand in front of her face. "I need you to focus. What just happened there?"

"Sorry." Kira forced a smile on her face. Just because the GM was paying her a personal visit didn't mean anything negative. *Maybe he was coming to tell her what a great job she was doing. Or just making a routine site visit.* There were a million reasons he would come out to Riverside. "I was just thinking of something." She shook her head clear of any worry and asked Sasha, "Why would the GM be here? Did he say?"

Sasha's face twisted up in confusion. "The GM? He's not here. Although I did—"

A spark of panic lit in Kira's belly, followed by something else. A feeling she couldn't quite pin down. She froze and stared at Sasha. "Then who's here?"

"I guess I thought you knew," Sasha said. A hot shiver

ran up her spine, and in that instant Kira knew. She *felt* it. She turned as Sasha continued. "He said he was your—"

"Brother." Kira's lips formed around the word while her eyes took in the scene before her. *Kade.*

Behind her, Sasha was saying something, but Kira didn't even try to understand what she was saying. A low-grade buzzing took over her hearing, the earth beneath her feet started to move, and for one terrifying moment, she thought she might pass out. *What was Kade doing there? How did he even know where she was? How could he…had he sensed her?*

Her knees buckled, but she caught herself and straightened. To his credit, Kade didn't try to help her or even move from the place he stood. He knew her well enough to know that she'd hate any kind of assistance at that moment.

He *had* known her well enough. She corrected herself. He didn't know her anymore. They hadn't seen each other in almost two years. He no longer had the right to say how she would react and how she wouldn't.

Except he did. He was her twin. A bond stronger than any other. Even that of a fated mate. It didn't matter what they'd been through, or the time they spent apart. He knew her. Kade *knew* her on a cellular level because they were twins.

"Kira." He finally spoke, and the sound of his voice speaking her name almost undid her completely. "You look good," he continued. "Happy."

He knew.

How could he know? It was a stupid thing to wonder. *After all, how could Kade know anything after so much time?*

Because he did. Her thoughts flew to Nash and what they'd just done. What would her brother say if he knew she'd just mated with a *wolf?* Did she even care?

Yes. She did. A lot.

"I am happy." She took a step forward, needing to touch him to really believe it was him. Sensing her need—maybe feeling it too—Kade stepped forward as well until they were toe-to-toe. "You're happy, too." It wasn't a question. It didn't need to be. He was radiating joy. But in a different way than she'd ever felt from him. It was pure, and heated and... "You have a mate."

Kade's face twisted into a broad smile. "There's time for that later." He laughed. "First things first." His broad, strong arms wrapped around her waist and she squealed as he lifted her up and spun her around.

As soon as she was able to wriggle her arm free, Kira swatted at him half-heartedly. "Put me down. I'm too big for that."

"You are not." And to demonstrate, he lifted her higher.

"Okay, okay. But I'm not a kid anymore." She smacked his back with a laugh. "Put me down."

Kade did as requested but then pulled her in for another hug. "Damn, sis. It's good to see you. I can't even—"

"You don't have to say it. I get it." And she did. Seeing Kade, hearing his voice, feeling his arms around her...he filled a hole deep inside her. It was a hole she didn't even realize she had, but now that he was there in front of her, she felt complete in a way that she couldn't explain. "It's been too long." Her voice was muffled by his shoulder. "Why now?"

Kade held her out from him so she was looking into his eyes. "You tell me."

It had to be last night. When she thought of him. When, even for a moment, she'd reached out to him. *But how could he get there so fast?* She shook her head. "No. It's impossible. There's no way. Not even you could travel that fast."

"What are you talking about?"

"Last night. I..." She caught herself, remembering they

weren't alone. "Hey, Sasha?" Kira turned to see her friend watching them with wide eyes. "Can you do me a huge favor?"

Sasha laughed. "I'll cover for you. But you owe me."

"Of course. Thank you."

"No problem." Sasha walked close, and lowered her voice. "But you're going to have to explain to me how you've had such a hot brother that you didn't bother telling me about. Damn, girl, that's not the type of thing you keep from a friend."

Kira laughed and looked to her brother, who, judging by the humor reflected in his face, had heard Sasha loud and clear.

They waited until she went back inside and Kira grabbed her brother's hand. "Come on. I want to talk to you, but we should probably get away from this."

Kade nodded. "No other shifters around here?"

Nash's face flashed in her mind, but she squeezed her eyes. "No." She lied to her brother. "Just me."

They each took an ATV and Kira drove them out past the campsites, to where the river curved. It wasn't totally secluded but it was far enough away from people that they could talk. And man, did they have a lot to talk about.

Kira had to bite back the growing guilt she had for lying about Nash. No doubt Kade would be able to sense the shift in her, just as she had with him. A topic she was definitely going to get back to just as soon as she could. But for him. Not her. She couldn't explain it, but she didn't want to tell her brother about Nash. Not yet. She needed to feel things out first, see where he stood on everything. Mainly, accepting her back into the clan.

Was that even possible?

Would her family welcome her back?

Could she *go* back?

For too long, Kira had erased the hope that she would ever be able to go home. It seemed like such an unattainable goal. How could she ever go home if they didn't want her? But now, he was here. *Why now?*

"Why now?" Kira fired off the question the second she'd shut off the ATV and before Kade had even swung his leg over to stand. "Why are you here? Why now?" she asked again. Kira hated that she could feel the tears building in her eyes. She didn't want to cry. Not now. Not in front of Kade. She shook her head and looked away, forcing herself to calm down as emotions rolled through her.

"Kira."

She could feel him. Sense him, right behind her. "I don't know what to say."

Kira spun around. "Tell me why." Anger she didn't know she was holding onto flew out of her. "Tell me how you could have turned your back on me like I was gone forever."

"You were." His anger matched hers. "You chose *him*." Kade's words were like a dagger through her heart. It was too easy to remember the pain of that day as her brothers walked away. "Do you have any idea how it tore me up inside to stand by and do nothing while you made that mistake? It *killed* me, Kira. It shredded me." His handsome face twisted; his eyes darkened as he recalled the day. "And yes, I walked away," he continued. "Because it was what you wanted. I would have done anything for you. I still would," he added more softly. "You're my sister. My *twin* sister. That means everything. And I know now that I did the right thing because I can see your happiness. I can feel it."

Guilt flooded through her. She was happy. But not for the reasons Kade thought. She had to tell him the truth. "I am happy." She looked down at her feet and kicked a rock. "But I'm not with Ryan anymore."

"What? But he's your mate, Kira. Your fated mate and I know how that—"

"He's not." She looked up, ashamed to look her brother in the eyes, but she forced herself. "He fooled me. It wasn't real."

"But it...you said..."

"I know what I said." For the second time, she had to blink back tears. *Damn. It was easier to be mad.* "But I was wrong. It wasn't real. None of it. He used me to further some sort of stupid family vendetta against Grandpa that apparently was only important to him. It was all so stupid and—"

Kade gripped her upper arms and shook her. "Why didn't you come home? Why did you stay away?"

She couldn't do it. She couldn't hold back the tears any more. She didn't look away as the tears spilled over her cheeks. "You didn't want me, Kade. I wanted to. But only if you all wanted me back."

"Of course we wanted you back! When you left, you took a piece of me, Kira. You must feel that, too."

She nodded. Of course she felt it. She'd felt it every damn day for far too long. "I tried to reach out to you, Kade." She sniffed and tried desperately to make herself stop crying. "Every night, I'd run in the forest and reach out. But you weren't there." A sob escaped her throat as she remembered those early days of loneliness and desperation. "But you weren't there, Kade. It was unlike anything I'd ever experienced before. It was like instead of you, there was a big black hole. It was so...*empty*."

"Kira, I—"

"No." She shook her head. She needed to get it all out. "I tried and tried, Kade. Every night for months. But you

100

were never there. It was like you were gone. Totally and completely gone. I was alone."

He dropped his hands from her arms and looked to the ground. After a moment, Kade looked up again, his own eyes shining with tears. "I'm sorry, Kira. I'm so sorry."

"Why didn't you want me?"

"It's not that I didn't. It was the exact opposite. It hurt too much to miss you, and the one thing that had caused that pain was the same thing that had broken our family the first time. Mates. I couldn't think straight and the only thing I could focus on was the fact that the very thing we were had destroyed us. I wanted no part of it."

"Part of what? Being a bear?" Kira struggled to wrap her mind around what he was saying. "But that's who you are. It's part of you, Kade. You can't get away from it."

"I know that now. But it didn't stop me from trying." He chuckled and shook his head, but it wasn't funny.

It was anything but funny. *Had Kade tried to deny his bear? The same way she had?* Maybe they'd been more connected than she'd thought. Only for males it was different. When she denied her bear, it just dulled her senses and instincts. The longer she went ignoring her true self, the farther away it became, which was why Nash had trouble identifying that she was even a shifter.

But when a male shifter denied his true self, it could eat him up. It could change a man. Maybe even drive him a little mad. It must have been torture for him. "But now..."

"Now I'm better." Kade's grin told her there was a lot more to do with him being *better* than he was saying, but she didn't push. There'd be time to catch up on all the details later. At least she hoped there would. "It's been a few months, Kira," he continued. "But I've been looking for you. Searching. But when I reached out to you, I couldn't—"

"I denied my bear, too." She dropped her head, but he lifted it and forced her to look at him. There was humor in his eyes, but also sadness.

"It would be funny, if it wasn't so sad, wouldn't it?"

She nodded. They always had been more alike than they even realized.

"But…why? Why would you—"

"You know why." She didn't have to wait long for realization to fill Kade's eyes.

"Because you couldn't reach me."

She nodded.

"And then I couldn't reach you." He shook his head and laughed for real. "Kira, we're a fuckin' mess."

She joined in his laughter because there was nothing else to do and she definitely couldn't disagree with him. "But you're here now," she said when she could find her words again. "What changed?"

"I found a mate." His smile transformed him. She'd never before seen her brother look so…giddy. It was the most ridiculous word to apply to Kade, who was a six-foot-three, solid mass of mountain man muscle, but there was really no other way to explain the look in his eyes. He was positively gleeful. "I can't wait for you to meet her, Kira. You're going to love her. She's….she's absolutely everything. And she helped me realize that by denying my bear, I was denying every part of me that mattered. Including you."

A completely unreasonable spark of jealousy flashed through her. As his twin sister, she should have been there to help him make that realization. It was her job.

But it wasn't.

And it was her fault that he'd denied his true self in the first place. Besides that, if she could look past the jealousy, she could see the truth for what it was. Nash had done the very same thing for her.

"I'm so glad, Kade." She squeezed him in a hug. "I can't wait to meet this woman," she said genuinely. "She must be pretty fantastic to lock down the first Jackson brother."

Kade's eyes clouded and he shook his head. "I keep forgetting." Her joy was gone in a flash, twisting instead into a tight knot. "You don't know."

"What don't I know?"

"We should go back," Kade said. "Maybe have a cup of coffee and talk."

"No." She shook her head. "Talk to me, Kade." Her hand latched around his arm, and she pulled. Kade was strong, but she could hold her own with her brother. Especially where her family was concerned. "What's happened at home?"

CHAPTER TEN

Nash had been looking for Kira everywhere. When he'd let her slip off to work without pulling her back into his bed to ravish her one more time, he'd only been able to muster the self-control because he was sure he'd be able to have her only a few hours later. Because that's all he could think about. Being with her. Feeling her skin on his. Her kiss on his lips. The sound of her voice.

He was addicted.

And he needed a fix. But he couldn't find her anywhere.

He'd avoided asking Sasha or any of the others whether they knew where she was because he didn't want to appear needy or possessive. But damn it, he was. He needed to possess her. In every way. The woman had completely gotten under his skin and he didn't want her to leave. Ever.

But he did need to cool it, at least for the time being.

He glanced toward the parking space where Kira's ATV was usually parked. It was still gone. As well as the spare one.

Settle down, Nash. She's fine.

He'd assumed mating would have lessened the urgency in his veins to be with her, but it had only increased it. Of course, he could be feeling plain old-fashioned desire for his woman. He laughed at himself. That's exactly what it was. He was just a man who wanted his woman. Nothing unusual there.

There was only one thing that could possibly take his mind off Kira, and fortunately for him, his brother chose that exact moment to call him. Any other day, and Nash would have avoided the call, but the distraction was desperately needed. He grabbed his cell phone off the front seat of the truck and headed out into the sunshine of the day before he picked up.

"Nolan," he answered his brother. "I don't suppose you're calling to invite me for Fourth of July celebrations?"

"Depends. Have you sorted your shit out yet?"

Nash shook his head. *How did he know the conversation was going to go that way?*

"I'm sure you'd say that I haven't, brother." But as far as Nash was concerned, he'd sorted everything out just fine. "I do wish you'd change your mind on all of this, though. I'd love to see you."

It wasn't a lie. Despite their disagreements, he truly missed his brother.

There was a long pause, followed by an exhale. "Have you chosen a mate?"

Nash knew what Nolan was really asking. He wanted to know whether Nash had decided to take what he deemed an *acceptable* mate. There was a big difference as far as Nash was concerned. Hell. An even bigger difference now than it had been only a day ago.

He took a deep breath of his own before he answered. "What if I told you I had?"

"Then you better tell me that your female is pure-blooded, from an appropriate pack, Nash." Nolan didn't even hesitate in his answer. "Because that's the only answer that will be acceptable and that is the only way you'll be welcomed back into the pack, brother. And you know it."

He did know it. Man, did he ever. The thought had gone through his head the night before, but it hadn't mattered. Not when Kira was in front of him, with everything she represented to him and their future together. It was no contest. If asked, he'd admit that the thought of never seeing his brother or going home again hurt. A lot. But it was a small price to pay. And the moment he told Nolan the truth, it would seal his fate. Forever.

He swallowed hard, but there was no hesitation when he opened his mouth and said, "My mate is a bear. A grizzly." Nolan didn't answer immediately. Not that Nash expected him to. He waited a beat, and then two. Finally, Nash said, "I don't expect you to understand, brother."

"That's a damn good thing," Nolan scoffed.

"I know you—"

"You don't know a fucking thing." His brother was only barely controlling his anger, and even then, not very well. "You don't know a goddammed thing, little brother. Not a thing." A growl rumbled through the line and Nash was happy he wasn't standing in front of Nolan. Although fairly evenly matched in size and stature, an alpha wolf was nothing to be messed with. Nash was coming into his own as an alpha, but even then, he had no desire to get into it with his brother. And definitely not in Nolan's current state.

"I know that I love her." Nash kept his voice even and as calm as possible. "I couldn't fight it, Nolan. I can't even begin to explain it."

"Well, you better try, little brother. Because when I see you, I'm going to tear your fucking head off. You have a *duty* to this pack. You mate and breed with a pure bred. You further the bloodline. It's what you do, Nash."

"It's not what I do."

"It is!" The growl that came through the line more than made Nolan's point. "Renounce her," he demanded.

Renounce? Hell no. He'd only heard of it in passing before. It occurred when a pair mated and then decided it was a mistake. It didn't happen often and it was absolutely not going to happen with him and Kira.

"You must do it at once," Nolan continued. "It's not too late to fix it."

"No."

"Nash," Nolan snarled through the phone. "She's a bloody bear. It's not natural."

But it was. He knew he'd never be able to make his brother understand. Especially because Nolan *had* mated for duty and not love.

"No," he said again.

"Your duty is to further the bloodline, Nash."

"That's your job," he fired back.

"We can't."

"What?"

His brother sighed and repeated himself, softer this time. "We haven't been able to conceive a pup yet. The pack is in trouble, Nash. We need you."

Nash looked out over the river. He turned north, in the direction of his brother's pack. *His* pack. They needed him. He knew that. And through the anger, he could hear it in his brother's voice. He turned and looked toward the cabin, where less than twenty-four hours ago he'd mated with Kira.

"Nash. Are you there?"

He nodded and, when he realized his brother couldn't see him, he added, "I am."

"I'm asking you, brother. Make the right choice. For your future. The future of your pack. It's not too late. I'll be waiting."

Nash held the phone to his ear until he heard the dial tone signaling the disconnect.

Of course his pack needed him. But Kira needed him, too. He needed Kira. And their connection was too strong to break. He felt it in his veins. Nothing would be able to break them apart.

Not even family.

"Nash is looking for you." Sasha popped her head out of the check-in window as Kira walked by.

She was half hoping to go undetected after returning from her chat with Kade, but she knew there was a very slim chance of that happening. No doubt the entire staff was buzzing with the news that Kira had a visitor. Which meant that no doubt Nash would have already heard about Kade's arrival.

And why did that thought fill her with dread?

Not that she wasn't happy with Kade being there. She was. Hell, she was thrilled. She had her brother back. But then why did the idea of introducing her grizzly bear brother to her alpha male mate, who happened to also be a wolf, terrify her? It didn't make sense that she should be so happy and so scared all at the same time.

But she was.

And it did make sense.

She was a bear.

Nash was a wolf.

Kade wouldn't understand.

"Hello?" Sasha waved her hand. "Did you hear me?"

"I did." Kira smiled at her friend, although she was positive it didn't reach her eyes. "Sorry. I just have so much to think about right now. What's going on?"

Sasha gave her a strange look. "Nash is looking for you.

Did you find him?"

She hadn't. But she also hadn't been looking. On one hand, her entire body yearned to be with her mate, but from the moment she'd seen Kade, she'd forced that part of her to be quiet and settle down.

"No," she said. "Do you know where he is?" Maybe if she could go see him wherever he was and keep him away from her brother, at least until she could figure out how to tell Kade about her mate without having him go off the deep end, that would be the best situation. After all, she'd just gotten her brother back; she didn't think she'd be able to survive losing him again so soon. And she would lose him. It was bad enough when she'd run off to choose Ryan, who *was* a bear, albeit one from the *wrong* clan. If her family found out she'd mated with a wolf, they'd surely disown her once and for all. She'd not only lose Kade, but *all* her brothers. And their mates. Her *sisters.*

Kade had filled her in on everything that had happened since she'd been gone and it had been a lot. First, her oldest brother Axel had fallen in love and mated. And then Luke. And Kade. Her own twin had found his mate and she hadn't known. It filled her with joy at the thought of her brothers being happy, but also sadness. She'd missed it all. When Kade told her Axel and his mate Harper had just had a cub, a little girl, she almost exploded from the excitement. She was an *aunt.* It was all too much. She couldn't wait to get up to Montana and see everyone.

Nash.

"Kira?" Sasha smacked her palm against the glass to get her attention. "Seriously. Are you listening to a word I'm saying?" Kira blinked hard and tried not to look too out of it. "I just told you he was up at the south shower house. Another clogged drain to deal with."

"I'll go find him there, thanks."

"Aren't you going to tell me about your brother?"

Kira smiled. "He's not single."

"Damn."

Kira laughed. She was used to women being ridiculously attracted to her brothers. It had been happening since they were teenagers. "In fact, he brought his ma—girlfriend with him." She corrected herself quickly. She hadn't met Kade's mate yet, but she was looking forward to it, just as soon as she found Nash and...*what?* She didn't know yet. "Anyway, I should get going. I think I'll go check on the progress of those clogged drains."

Sasha wiggled her eyebrows. "You do that."

CHAPTER ELEVEN

"I was hoping to find you here."

Kira hoped her voice sounded natural as she walked up behind Nash, who was loading his toolbox into the back of the truck. He turned and gave her such a sexy smile that all the concerns she had only moments ago disappeared.

"Hey, babe." He slid his arms around her and pulled her close. "I've been looking for you all day. Where've you been?"

Instead of answering him, she kissed him. The slightest touch of his lips on hers fired her internal fire and her bear both settled inside her while at the same time, demanded more from her mate.

"I've been crazy busy today." It wasn't a lie, but she still felt guilty. "What's happening here? Everything under control?"

Nash shook his head. A frown slipped over his handsome face. "No. I mean, I fixed the clog. But when I was doing a routine check, I noticed one of the shower heads wasn't flowing properly. Turns out there was a cracked pipe in the wall. I had to shut the entire system down."

"Down? What does that mean? Is it operational?" Kira

instantly slipped into manager mode. If the shower house was down, it meant they would have double the capacity at the north shower house and it was definitely not designed to handle that capacity. Which meant one thing: pissed-off campers.

"It's not." Nash shook his head. "I have to go to West Yellowstone to get parts. It's just outside the gates."

"I know where it is."

He smiled, and she realized she probably sounded edgy, so she offered him a smile in return.

"Until then, I have to close it off."

The smile vanished. "What?" She bit her lip. "Now?"

"I'm sorry, babe." He stroked her cheek. "Don't worry about it though, okay? I'll get it fixed as fast as I can. It will hardly be a disruption." He stopped talking and gave her a strange look. "You look stressed. Please don't worry about this, okay?"

Kira shook her head and pulled away from his arms. As much as she wanted his touch, first she needed to tell him about Kade. "It's fine," she said. "I know you'll get it fixed as soon as you can. I'm not worried about the shower."

"Then what?" He reached out, but she stepped aside. "What's going on, Kira? You're scaring me."

"Sorry." She forced a smile. "I'm not trying to scare you. Actually, it's a good thing." She took a breath. "My brother is in town, and I thought maybe you could meet him but if you have to go—"

"Your brother?"

The rest of the words she was going to babble froze on her lips and she nodded.

"He's here?" Nash's eyes widened as he took in what she was saying. "At the campground?" She nodded. "Your brother, Kade?"

Kira nodded again.

"But I thought you didn't speak? I thought your twin connection or whatever wasn't working."

"It wasn't." She shrugged. It was too much to get into right now. "But it is now. He's here."

Nash's face split into his trademark grin and he pulled her back into a hug. "Babe, that's fantastic. You must be thrilled."

She was thrilled. She couldn't even process how good it felt to have her brother back. But she was also terrified. Because she hadn't really been sure she was going to tell Nash about him and now that she had, it felt amazing because she wanted to tell him everything, always. But it was equally scary because now he'd want to meet Kade and then...well, she couldn't think about it. Not yet. Because no matter what, she would not lose her brother again. Now that she had filled that missing piece of her heart, Kira knew with certainty that she would never be able to survive the loss a second time.

"I am," she answered after a moment. "And I really wish you could meet him, but now you have to go to West Yellowstone and get that piece."

"No."

"No?"

"Well, of course I have to go, but it can wait a few minutes. Let's go back to the office now, I should grab a quick overnight bag anyway, and then I can at least meet him. I mean, he's your brother, Kira. Your *twin*. I think I can find a few minutes to meet my mate's brother. Don't you?"

She nodded with a smile pasted on her face and hoped Nash hadn't noticed the way she flinched at the use of the word mate.

Nash followed Kira's ATV back to the main offices and tried to shake off the feeling that something was wrong. Very wrong. It wasn't just that Kira didn't seem as excited as he would have thought, with her brother there, but it was something else. He couldn't pinpoint it, but something was off. It was probably just the shock of Kade showing up. After all, they hadn't seen each other in almost two years and as far as Kira was concerned, would likely never see him again. Of course it would be shocking for him to show up with no announcement. And then, of course, there was everything that had happened between the two of them.

Damn. It had definitely been an eventful few days.

Nash chuckled to himself as he reasoned it out. Of course Kira seemed a little preoccupied. The last twenty-four hours had been intense, to say the least.

A few minutes later when they pulled up behind the offices, everything made perfect sense to Nash. He pulled her into his arms and gave her a quick, hard kiss that he hoped expressed his love and support for her. She melted into it, and when he pulled away, the sparkle was back in her eyes.

"Babe, you know I'm here for you." He squeezed her hand. "Whatever you need, okay?"

"Thank you." She smiled. "You go pack your things and I'll get Kade, okay? Meet me back here in ten?"

"Make it five. I'll be right back."

Her smile wavered, but she agreed, so Nash didn't push it. Instead, he gave her one more kiss on the cheek and took off into the cabin. He was only inside a few minutes, but when he returned, Kira was already there, sitting at the picnic tables behind the offices with a man and a woman. Nash dropped his duffel bag by the door and strode over to the small group.

Kira stood the moment she saw him. Her smile was strained, and once again she looked worried.

"Hey, ba—"

"Nash." She smoothly interrupted him and sidestepped his arm, clasping her hands together in front of her as he joined her next to the table. "There you are." Her eyes wouldn't meet his. Her voice was high and tight. "I want you to meet my brother, Kade." She pointed to the man, which was completely unnecessary. The family resemblance was clear.

Nash looked the man in the eyes and shook his hand. There was a flash of something in Kade's eyes, a thread of tension in his handshake. No doubt he recognized him as a shifter. *How much had Kira told him?*

"It's good to meet you, Kade. I've heard a lot about you."

"I can't say the same."

There it was. The tension turned slightly to animosity. Nash released his hand.

Before he could say anything, Kira was making the introduction to the woman who stood next to Kade. "And this is Kade's ma—fiancée, Ella."

"It's nice to meet you, Ella." The woman had a warm smile and even warmer demeanor. It only took a quick shake of her hand for Nash to know he was going to get along just fine with Ella. It was Kira's brother who was definitely going to be the problem.

"I just met Ella myself." Kira was babbling. "It's been kind of crazy around here today. First Kade shows up, and then the showers. Never mind everything else, and I haven't even thought about the fish problem yet."

Her face was lined with tension, and Nash wanted nothing more than to go to her and pull her into his arms and tell her not to worry, that everything would be okay. But he couldn't. Something was off.

"Where are you from, Nash?" Kade was still staring at him. "And what is it you do around here?"

He knew exactly what the man was asking him, and Kira's long-lost brother or not, Nash was not one to back down. "I don't think where I'm from or what it is that I do is nearly as important as who I am to Kira."

Protectiveness and anger flashed in Kade's eyes at the exact moment that Kira jumped between them. "Would anyone like a bottle of water?"

Nash and Kade shook their heads at the same time.

"I want to know what Nash was going to say." Kade's hard gaze didn't leave his. "Who is he to you, Kira?"

She swallowed hard, and Nash could see the struggle on her face. She closed her eyes briefly and when she opened them again, she stared directly at her brother. "Nash is the maintenance man at Riverside. He's also a friend."

Friend. The word sliced through his heart. Kira wouldn't look at him. She'd called him a *friend.* After what they'd done last night. With her arm likely still sore and throbbing from the evidence of their mating, and she'd stood in front of her brother and denied him. Her *mate.*

Nash choked on the growl that threatened to escape his lungs.

"Kira?"

Still, she wouldn't look at him. He waited a beat. And then another.

"Don't you have some work to do?" The question came from Kade, but he ignored him for the moment, his eyes fixed on his mate. He could see her jaw tremble, her knuckles white where she clenched her hands together. Finally, she turned to him.

Seeing the pain in her eyes, he wanted to go to her and

shake her. Growl at her. Whatever it took to figure out what the fuck had just happened. But he was aware of their audience.

Mustering as much composure as he could, Nash said, "Well, it was nice to meet you both." It was a lie, and they all knew it. "But I should get going if I'm going to get to West Yellowstone to pick up the parts for the shower. I just have a few questions. Kira, would you mind walking me to the truck so we can go over a few things?"

Kira kept her eyes fixed forward on the trees as she walked. She couldn't look at him. He was going to be mad.

No.

He *was* mad. She could feel the anger radiating off him as he walked next to her. They didn't touch. They didn't talk. Not yet.

Besides the anger, there was something else coming from him.

Pain.

She felt it as acutely as if it were her own. Because it was.

Together, they turned the corner around the building and then they were alone, away from the prying eyes of Kade and his mate Ella. Kira didn't doubt for a moment that they'd be watching closely. The way her brother had reacted when he met Nash—no doubt he sensed something.

Had she made the wrong choice not telling the truth?

She lifted her head and, for the first time since they'd walked away, looked at Nash.

Yes. She'd made the wrong choice.

"Nash, I need to—"

"What was that all about?" His words were controlled,

but only barely. She could see the fire flash in his eyes, his animal contained just below the surface. "What the hell was that about?" He demanded an answer and more than anything, she wanted to give him one.

"I need you to understand." Tears pricked at her eyes, but she wouldn't cry.

"I'm trying, Kira. But for the life of me, I can't think of one fucking reason why you would put me through that. I am your mate," he growled. "And you treated me no better than a fucking employee." He turned on his heel and stamped a few feet away before he turned around again and stalked toward her.

Reflexively, Kira stepped backward until her back hit the side of the building. He was inches from her. The anger and hurt darkened his gray eyes, intensifying his energy. "Tell me," he demanded. His hands pressed up on the wall on either side of her head, caging her in. "Tell me why you would deny me."

Her stomach knotted and twisted, torn between her mate—her love—and her brother and the promise of family. She'd seen the way Kade had reacted to Nash and that was before he knew the truth. He'd tear him apart if he knew Nash was her mate. He'd walk away forever. The sister-in-law she'd only just met, the promise of her other brothers' mates, Axel's new cub….it would be gone. The family she'd just found would be taken from her.

This time, forever.

But Nash…

A sob caught in her throat but she swallowed it back, hard. *Nash was everything. How could she walk away?* It was an impossible choice.

"Kira." Some of the anger faded from his voice. "Talk to me. What happened back there?"

She shook her head. "I…I have a family."

Nash nodded. "I gathered."

"No." She desperately needed him to understand. "You don't get it. My brothers all have mates now. My oldest brother has a cub. A cub." Nash nodded, but she could see he didn't understand. Not really. "When I left, it was just the four of us and then when I thought they were gone forever, I forced myself not to care."

"But you do."

She nodded. "I do. My family, they mean..." She trailed off. *How could she stand in front of her mate and tell him that her family meant everything to her?* Just like her choice would be made. Maybe it already was.

Her arm throbbed and ached from his bite, and she couldn't find the words. She couldn't make a choice.

"And if you tell them you're mated to a wolf..." Nash picked up her arm and pulled it high over her head where his pinned it to the wall, so his mark was exposed. Kira knew if she turned her head, she'd see the mark of their love. Hot tears slipped from her eyes and she turned away. Nash lowered his head and traced the tender mark with his tongue. Kira's entire body quivered from the intensity of his touch. "If you tell them you bare the mark of a mate..." Nash kissed the center of his claim before raising his head. With his free hand, he turned her head and forced her to look at him. "They won't accept your choice." It wasn't a question, but Kira nodded.

He kept her arm pinned over her head; his free hand held her under the chin, forcing her eyes on his. She saw the anger change to understanding, but the hurt never faded.

"Nash, I—"

He shook his head to stop her words. "We all make choices."

"But, Nash. I—"

"I think it's time I told you about my brother and my pack."

He'd only spoken vaguely about his pack and how the wolves differed from bears. Nash had never seemed open to discussing his family and she'd never pushed.

"It's imperative to our pack that we increase our numbers," Nash started. "After being reintroduced to Yellowstone, we got a chance we never thought we would and now the only focus for my family is to reproduce."

She nodded. It was a familiar story for many shifter families.

"Remember when I told you we didn't have fated mates?"

She nodded again.

"That's only because in my pack, we don't choose our own mates. They're chosen for us." He'd told her that part before and although not an ideal situation, it was also a fairly common practice among shifters. It was, in fact, part of the reason Kira's own mother had been cast out of their clan by her grandfather. "I've always known that's how it was," Nash continued. "And part of me didn't really mind, but when it came time, I decided I needed space. So I left."

"That's why you're here."

Nash nodded. "He made it clear when I left that I wouldn't be welcomed back unless I was willing to play by his rules. I think I always thought on some level that I'd go back and take a mate the way my brother wanted me to. I never thought I'd actually stay away. Not forever anyway." He reached out and stroked a finger down her cheek. "And then I met you."

Kira's knees buckled beneath her, but Nash held her strong.

"From the moment I laid eyes on you, I knew you were mine." He stared straight into her eyes, challenging her to say differently. She couldn't. Despite the way she'd fought it, she'd felt it, too. "I knew what taking you for my mate would mean to my family and my future. But that's what I chose."

A sob rose in her throat at the knowledge that he did for her the exact thing she wasn't sure she could do for him.

"Kira, I love you." His lips brushed hers. "You're my world, my heart, my *mate*. Without you, I have nothing. But I will never ask you to choose between me and your family. If it's a choice you have to make, I won't stand in your way. But I won't lie to you and tell you it'll be okay. It won't. Every moment without you by my side will shred me from the inside out." He pressed his mouth to hers and kissed her with a heat that threatened to consume them both. Kira's body lit up in response, her animal rising to the surface. It was a kiss of possession and ownership, but also, one of good-bye. When he pulled back, his gray eyes were clouded, the feeling unreadable. "You are my life, Kira. But if it's what you want, I love you enough to let you go."

And then he did. He released her arm, letting it slide down the wall to her side, and he stepped back.

"Nash." She took a step forward, but he shook his head, halting her.

"I'll go to town and I'll be back in a few days. The extra time will be good. For both of us. If you decide this is what you want, I will renounce you and you'll be free."

His words sliced through her heart. She didn't want that. The very thought of being without him gutted her. It was an impossible choice. She wanted to tell him no. She wanted to stop him before he walked away and tell him that she chose him. Always. It would always be him.

"I'll see you in a few days."

She couldn't look at him as he walked away from her

and got in the truck. She fell to her knees and as he drove away from her, she could no longer control the sobs that racked her body.

Somehow Kira managed to get through the rest of the afternoon. After Nash left, she didn't go back to where she'd left Kade and Ella. Instead, she went into the cabin, splashed some water on her face, retied her hair into a tighter braid and went to work for a few hours. She needed to lose herself in the daily concerns of running a campground in a busy national park. Anything to take her mind off Nash. And the fact that her life was once again crumbling around her.

Her distraction technique worked pretty well, too. If anyone wondered why she wanted to take the closing shift at the customer service window, they didn't ask. Thankfully, everyone stepped aside and let Kira handle the busywork of checking guests into their sites, selling campfire wood, and dealing with a few minor complaints.

"I'm sorry, Mrs. Bruce, we don't have any river-side campsites available," she lied to the woman who had specifically requested a riverfront site six months ago when she'd booked the busy campground. "But I do have one of our nicest spots available. It's a lovely forested spot and you're very lucky since the reservation just canceled this morning." Kira couldn't believe her luck, but she wasn't about to question it. There was no way she would be giving out the riverfront campsites until they had the whole dead fish thing figured out. And the last she heard, there'd been another bunch of fish found that morning. Sasha had tried to keep it from her, but secrets didn't last long in the office.

"Do you have any idea how early I had to book in order to get a riverfront spot?" Mrs. Bruce didn't seem to be as happy with her site change as Kira had hoped. "I had to wake up at five in the morning, six months ago, to get this site reserved and now you're telling me it's not available?"

Kira tried her best to look as if she cared about the woman's problem, but all she really wanted to do was tell her where she could shove her complaints. Maybe she should give her the stinky dead fish site after all? Maybe that would make Mrs. Bruce happy. But she didn't. Because she needed the job.

Or did she?

She hadn't had a chance to talk about it with Kade and Ella yet, but she'd just assumed she'd go home to Jackson Valley or the new guest ranch her brothers had set up, Grizzly Ridge. Yes, she really wanted to visit Grizzly Ridge and all her brothers. But stay there?

Without Nash?

The decisions and questions she couldn't answer crashed through her head again.

"Are you even listening to me?" Mrs. Bruce tapped her hand on the counter to get her attention.

"Yes," Kira lied. "Of course I am." She took a breath and tried her best to look composed. "I'll be honest with you, Mrs. Bruce. We do have one riverfront site available. But there have been mischief reports there lately and the sighting of dead fish. We're working hard to sort out the problem and in the meantime, I know how important your family vacation is to you and how long you've been planning it, so I thought you might like to avoid any unnecessary drama and stay at one of our finest treed spots. But if you insist on the original booking, I will honor it."

The woman's face shifted as she very clearly saw what was on offer. *Finally.* Pretty soon, she smiled and nodded. "The treed spot will be lovely."

Kira finished processing the check-in, passed on all the

pertinent information and closed her window behind Mrs. Bruce. The day was over. And that meant she couldn't avoid reality much longer. She'd agreed to join Kade and Ella at their campground for some dinner and she had less than an hour before she was going to be late.

She had enough time to change out of her uniform and into jeans and a t-shirt at the cabin, and was just about to slip out the door when Sasha stopped her.

"You've been busy today," her friend said, somewhat accusingly.

She didn't know why, but Kira felt a flash of guilt. "Sorry, Sasha. I really didn't expect my brother to show up. We haven't actually spoken in almost two years. I never would have….well, it's all been kind of crazy."

"And Nash?" Sasha tilted her head and gave Kira a wink that could only be interpreted one way. She knew Sasha meant well with her tease, but her friend had no idea that Kira had just let the love of her life walk away without even a word. It was too much. But she couldn't get into it with Sasha. She wouldn't understand the intricacies of the situation and as much as she wished she had someone to confide in, she didn't. Not the way she needed to.

Kira forced a sliver of a smile and hoped it was enough to satisfy Sasha.

"It's okay if you're busy, Kira. I get it and you know that's what we're here for."

Something about the way she said *we* caught her attention. "We?"

"Well…" Her friend blushed and looked down at her feet. "I just meant…well, Conner and me. That's what we're here for. To help you out."

Kira's lips curled up for real into a smile. "Sasha. Is there something you want to tell me?" She wiggled her eyebrow and when Sasha buried her face in her hands, Kira laughed. "No way," she said. "You and Conner?"

"No! I mean, yes. I mean...well, not really." She stumbled over her words. "It's just that...it's not...well, it's not that simple. But..."

"But yes?"

Sasha nodded. "Yes. It's still new. I mean, *really* new. But he's really not that bad at all. I mean, I don't think we gave him the benefit of the doubt before. You just have to get to know him."

"Clearly."

"I'm serious, Kira. I think he's just misunderstood. He's not perfect, and he has a few things he's trying to work out. And trust me, I'm the last person who expected anything to happen. But then we kept pulling shifts together, and spending more time talking and getting to know each other and..."

"And it just happened," Kira finished for her. "Really, I'm happy for you, Sasha. I don't understand it. But if you say he's a good guy then I believe you."

She listened to her friend for another few minutes before begging off to get ready for her dinner. Not that Kira minded the distraction, not at all. Talking to Sasha had definitely helped take her mind off Nash, but once she'd changed and was making her way down the path to Kade and Ella's campsite, the distraction had more than worn off. She tried to focus on all the positives of having Kade come back into her life. Because it *was* positive. It was freaking amazing. And with Ella and the others she hadn't even met yet. It was a dream come true.

So was Nash.

The problem was that both of her dreams had someone twisted into one monumental nightmare and more than anything, Kira wanted to wake up.

"Why so sad, *mi hermana?*"

Kira turned at the pretty Spanish accent and the use of the word sister.

"Oh, Ella. Sorry. I was lost in thought and...I'm not sad." The lie didn't sound remotely convincing, even to her own ears, and the look Ella gave her made it clear she didn't believe her either. Fortunately, she didn't push the issue.

Not at first.

"Come sit." Ella gestured her over to the picnic table. "We don't have much," she said. "And it must seem *muy diferente* to be having dinner at one of your own campsites. But I'm glad you came."

Kira smiled. She was glad too. Despite the circumstances. "Where's Kade?"

"He was a little wound up." Her smile dipped a little. "And now that he's rediscovered his bear, I find it's best for him to embrace it. It helps. *Mucho.*"

Kira couldn't argue with that. Ever since she'd started shifting again, she found the same thing. In fact, what she really needed, instead of sitting at a picnic table, was to get out into the woods and run off some steam. But she wouldn't be rude. Besides, maybe it wouldn't be so bad to spend a few minutes talking to someone who might be able to understand. Someone who wasn't her brother. And she was dying to get to know Ella a bit better.

"Going for a run is always a good idea," Kira said lamely.

"*Sí.* Especially with the *bebe* on the way."

Ella said it so casually, Kira couldn't be sure she'd heard right, but the smile on the other woman's face told her everything. "No way!" Kira jumped up from the picnic table and gave Ella a hug. "That's fantastic. I'm going to be an auntie again. I'm so excited." And she was, but the fact that her family was expanding just made her sad. Because that just made the choice harder. Or at least, more complicated. Kira returned to her seat at the table with a sigh.

"What's wrong, *mi amiga*?"

"I'm sorry, Ella. I don't mean to spoil your exciting news, but—"

"Your heart is broken. *Estas triste.*"

Ella's exacting diagnosis took her off guard. Kira's first reaction was to deny it, but there was no point. With a sigh, she dropped her head into her hands and rubbed her temples. "If I tell you something, will you promise not to tell Kade?" Not that she was able to keep secrets from him, but maybe just for a little while. Not that she had to worry, because Ella's smile gave her away.

"Tell me about your mate, *mi amiga.*"

Kira almost choked on the very air she breathed. "My mate?" There was no way she could know. *How would she have any idea...* Because she was a female. A female with a mate of her own. It was universal. "Nash." She spoke his name softly, because the very sound of it hurt her heart.

Ella nodded. "And that is the *problemo*? No?"

"Yes. He's a...he's not a bear."

Ella's hand reached across the table and squeezed her hand. "Love knows *sin limites*. No boundaries. No..."

"Species?" Kira laughed at the sound of it. But her laugh died on her lips because it was true. His species was the entire problem. Or was it hers? Either way, it *was* a problem. A very big problem. "Maybe you think love knows no species, but you're mated to my brother. He's a bear. That's different."

"*Como?*"

"Because...well...it's just that..." She sighed. "Because you're both bears. Nash is a wolf."

Ella squeezed her hand. "But it is love, no?"

Kira nodded.

"He is your mate? *Tu companero?*"

She nodded again. "Fated." The word came out as a whisper and Ella's eyes grew wide.

"*Predestinado?*"

Kira nodded. It was both scary and exciting to speak the word out loud. *It had to be fate.* She and Nash *were* fated. It felt like nothing less. "Yes. I mean, I think."

Ella let out a squeal and clapped her hands together. "If you think you are, then it is so. It's a feeling deep in your bones. There is no guessing. It is so."

"But I don't know." Kira dropped her head into her hands again. "I made that mistake once before." She didn't want to think about Ryan and Nash in the same thought but she couldn't help it. She'd thought once before she'd found her fated mate and there was no forgetting how that had turned out. It was the whole reason she was there in Yellowstone.

Where she met Nash.

"No," Ella said with the certainty Kira wished she felt. "It's not a mistake. You are fated. You are meant to be. I see it."

"You *see* it?"

"*Si.* Anyone can see it."

White-hot panic flooded through her and Kira jumped up from the table, unable to sit any longer. "Did Kade see it?"

Ella's laugh rang out through the campsite. "He's a man. He sees what he wants to. All he can see at the moment is his *hermana.*" She walked around the table and squeezed Kira's arm. "He is so happy you're here. That he has you back. He's a changed man."

Tears sprang to Kira's eyes and she wiped them away.

She was not a crier. In the last few days, she'd shed more tears than in the past few years and that included the hardest time of her life. But this was different. Everything was on the line now. Her life. Her future. Her happiness. Her love.

All of it. She just had to make a choice. *But which one?*

"Do not cry, *mi hermana*." Ella's soft touch wiped away a tear. "This is happy, no?"

She nodded and then shook her head. "No. It's not happy because I have to let him go. I have to renounce my mate. Or let him renounce me or however that works. I don't even know."

"No!" Ella's mouth fell open and horror lined her pretty face. "He is your fated mate, you told me so. Renouncing him will be *muerte*."

"Death?"

"To your soul." She clasped her hands to her chest. "To your heart. You must not let that happen."

She couldn't hold it in any longer. A sob so full of angst and pain rose up from inside her and burst out, dropping Kira to her knees. "But if I save my heart, I will lose my family and that will break me."

"No, no." Ella sat in the dirt next to her and pulled her close. "You will not lose your family if you choose love."

Kira snorted, and wiped her nose. "You don't understand my family. I will——"

"I understand your family very well, *mi hermana*. Very well. They are my family and they have accepted me with open arms."

She wanted to scream, Kira was so frustrated. Ella couldn't understand because she was a bear. The same as her mate. Maybe being from a different clan, a different country was troubling. But she was *still* a bear. Nash was a wolf. "He's a wolf, Ella. A *wolf*."

"Who's a wolf?"

Kira's blood froze in her veins.

Kade.

Next to her, Ella turned and looked over Kira's shoulder. Kira couldn't bring herself to look.

"Who's a wolf?" he asked again.

CHAPTER TWELVE

It had been late by the time Nash got to West Yellowstone the night before. He'd spent a restless night in the woods, running until his wolf was exhausted and he fell into a fitful sleep under a stand of trees. The next morning, he was no closer to having any answers when it came to Kira or what the hell he was going to do about his mate. By the time he fetched the part he needed for the showers and was back on the road to the campground, he'd been hoping to have some answers. Or at least some clarity.

He was wrong.

If anything, he was more fired up than ever.

She'd let him walk away.

What did you expect?

He couldn't answer that question. Because the only thing he *had* expected was for his mate to not let him walk away.

"Dammit!" He hit his hand on the steering wheel and pressed his foot to the gas at the same time, pushing the accelerator.

Why had he given her a choice? Why the fuck hadn't he grabbed her, pushed her up against the wall and told her exactly what was going to happen? Because what was going to happen was that he was going to go back to that campground, grab his mate, kiss her until she couldn't think of anything except the feel of him with her, on her and inside her, and then, only when she needed to come up for air, would he tell her exactly how things were going to be.

And how were they going to be?

"Dammit!" Again, he hit the steering wheel, and at the same time pushed the gas pedal harder.

Who was he fooling? He wasn't going to tell her anything. *No.* He wasn't going to barge back into that campsite and take her away from her family. *No.* He couldn't do that. And he wouldn't do that because when she had the chance, she didn't stop him.

Don't forget that.

He wouldn't forget that. Because that moment was seared in his mind forever. "Dammit, Kira."

His intersection approached, giving him a choice. If he went left, he'd be on the road to his brother and his pack. His family and everything he'd always known. He knew what Nolan wanted to hear. If he turned right, he'd go back to Riverside, to Kira and what? He told her he'd give her a few days. Besides, he wasn't ready for her to make the choice that could potentially shatter him. Not yet.

He took the left turn.

Nash had been driving the same roads his whole life, but every time he took the highway that led to his small village, nestled in the back side of Yellowstone, it was as if he were looking at it through new eyes. It changed so quickly. It was if the landscape were alive, always dancing with changes in the foliage and animals. This corner of the park didn't get as many tourists, which was why it had been a prime location for the reintroduction of the wolves. His pack lived a simple life, running the gas station, shops and small guest cottages there, but mostly they spent their days in the valley, running as wolves, allowing themselves to be spotted, just enough to keep the tourists happy. But not enough to threaten their way of life. The quiet life had always been enough for Nolan. But Nash could never shake the idea that there was more out there for him.

And there was.

There was Kira.

He tried to close his mind to thoughts of her, at least for the time being. Although there was nothing more that he wanted in his life, he couldn't have it if it wasn't what Kira wanted too. She needed to be sure of herself and her choices before she could have a life with him. Nash understood the calling of family and the need to be everything for them. That was the thing with shifters: it didn't matter what species you were. Family was first. Always. That was how he was raised; it was in his blood.

But that was before Kira.

His thoughts of her threatened to consume him, but fortunately for Nash, before that could happen, he turned in to the little village and pulled up in his old parking spot behind the souvenir shop.

He didn't know what to expect or even what he was hoping to get out of the visit. But he was there, and for better or worse, he needed to see his brother.

They were deep enough into the tourist season that people were milling about, taking photos, buying up souvenirs and making their plans for the day. Nash ignored all of them and walked into the store. The jingle of the bell over the door announced his presence. The woman behind the desk looked up with a smile on her face to greet her customer but the smile fell from her face when Julia recognized him.

"Nash."

"Hey, Julia." He'd always liked his brother's mate. She was a beautiful, tall blonde with a spirited streak that never failed to make Nash laugh. Especially when it was aimed at Nolan. Of course, what Nash used to think was playful banter between them, he now recognized as barely contained frustration. Nolan and Julia had been mated almost two years, and although it was not a relationship of choice, Nash had kind of assumed they'd grow to care about each other. The fact that the exact opposite seemed to be the case was the final straw for Nash when it came to making his choice to leave. The idea of being stuck in a relationship where he and his mate could barely stand the sight of each other filled him with dread. For the betterment of the pack or not, he just didn't think he could do it.

"What are you doing here?" Julia came around the counter and pulled him into a strong hug. "Does Nolan know you're here?" Her face lit up in hope, and Nash knew it was because she assumed he was back to stay.

"He doesn't."

"Are you here to—"

A quick shake of his head cut her off. "I just needed to see you guys. I need to get back to Riverside."

Disappointment lined her face. "I wish you'd come back, Nash." She squeezed his arms and released him. "Nolan misses you and…things are just getting worse."

He walked with her back to the counter and leaned against it while she went back to her post by the cash register. "What do you mean, worse?"

"He's just…he's so angry all the time and I know it's the stress, but it just makes things harder with us." For all the animosity between Julia and her husband, Nash knew there was something between them. It might not quite be love, and it may not be anything like what he had with Kira, but it was something. He could see it in Julia's eyes. "He needs you, Nash."

Guilt flooded him. "He needs me to have pups."

She nodded. "He does. *We* do. We all do, Nash. If we can't further our numbers…well, I don't know what will happen. It's important." A tear shone in her eye. "I should've been able to…well, it doesn't matter." She forced a smile. "I'm just happy to see you. And I know Nolan will be too."

Nash flashed her a smile. He knew all about Julia's fertility troubles; she didn't need him to press the issue and cause her more pain. "Where is my brother?" He still didn't know what he was going to say to Nolan, but he did know he needed to see his brother. However things would work out, he might as well get it over with.

The sky was gray when Kira woke in her empty bed, which matched her mood perfectly. She was no closer to feeling anything but confused and conflicted over her family and Nash. Two things which should have made her happier than anything else in the world, but all she could feel was pain.

The night before, she'd had the perfect opportunity to tell her brother about Nash. Ella would have supported her; she knew that. But when Kade stood there in front of her, asking what they were talking about, all Kira could think about was how much it would hurt if her brother turned his back and walked away from her again the way he had two years ago.

So she'd lied.

Well, not really. She just hadn't told him the whole truth.

"My maintenance man is a wolf," she'd told him.

The words had felt sour on her tongue, but when Kade's mouth twisted up in a snarl and he'd sneered, "I was sure I'd smelt dog," Kira knew she'd made the right choice not saying anything about Nash being her mate.

She'd heard Ella sigh behind her, when she changed the subject with her brother. No doubt the other woman was disappointed in her for not approaching the subject, but Ella didn't understand her situation. How could she possibly know what it would feel like to be in her predicament? Besides, they'd ended up having a great night. After a simple dinner around the campfire, Kade and Ella pulled out their phones and showed Kira photos of everyone back home. Through pictures, she got to see her brothers again. And meet their new mates. And the cub. *Oh, the cub.*

Just thinking of Axel and Harper's brand-new baby girl put a smile on Kira's face. She was an auntie to the most beautiful little baby girl and she absolutely couldn't wait to get that little sweetie in her arms for a snuggle.

That would be worth it.

Having her family back. It would be worth letting Nash go.

The pain hit her in the gut so hard and fast, it took her breath away completely. Kira curled tight into a ball and hugged her knees to her chest, willing the pain to subside. The pains had started sometime in the night, but only when she let herself think about the choice she had to make. After she'd left Ella and Kade and returned to the cabin, the decision had been clear. Or, at least clear enough. She couldn't let them go again.

It had been a long night.

Kira breathed through the pains and once they'd subsided enough that she could take in a breath without wanting to cry, she straightened and slid out of bed. She had a lot to do and prepare for if she was going to go back to Grizzly Ridge with Kade and Ella the next morning.

If she was going back.

"Pull yourself together, Kira." She tugged her hair back into a braid and pulled her shirt over her head. "This is everything you've ever wanted. This is a good thing."

And it was, on so many levels. She'd feel better about it once she started making the arrangements. And that's exactly what she was going to focus on. Not the pain in her gut that sliced through her with every breath.

A few hours later, and for the most part, Kira had managed to lose herself into the busywork in the office. She'd made the call to the head office to submit for emergency holiday time. They weren't typically permitted to take holidays during the busy summer season, but much to her surprise, human resources approved her request. She was just going to submit her resignation, because she knew that once she went home to Grizzly Ridge, she'd have a hard time leaving again. But she couldn't quite bring herself to close that door. Not yet.

The rest of the morning was spent making sure the schedules were made up and reservations were confirmed. Conner and Sasha had volunteered to do the rounds of the campground to be sure that guests had checked out on time and the sites were ready for new visitors. It was usually a job that Sasha tried her best to avoid, but apparently spending time with Conner had changed her opinion on a few things.

Kira shook her head, but couldn't help but smile. It was still hard to believe that Conner was worthy of Sasha's affections, but if her friend found good in the man, then Kira had to think there was something there she'd missed. Besides, as long as they were happy together, nothing else should matter.

Nothing else should matter.

Except sometimes things weren't as simple as all that and longing for it to be different wasn't going to change anything. "There's no point getting all worked up, Kira."

"Worked up about what?"

Kade appeared in the customer service window, his large frame filling it.

"I was just talking to myself."

"I figured that much." He laughed at her. "What were you saying?"

"I was just telling myself that there's no point in worrying about things you can't change." She tried to keep the sadness out of her voice, but judging by the look on her brother's face, she'd failed.

"What can't you change?"

She shrugged. "It's no biggie." She tried for a lighter tone when she added, "I was approved for my vacation time. I can leave with you guys tomorrow."

"About that. Can I talk to you, Kira?"

"Is everything okay?" *Had he found out about Nash? Had Ella told him she was mated to a wolf?* Her stomach knotted hard and if she hadn't caught herself on the desk, she was afraid her knees would have given out completely.

"It's all good," Kade said. "I just don't want to talk through the window."

"Of course." She waved him inside. A few moments later, he stood in the office with her. His large frame made the room feel much smaller than it was. "What's up?"

"I need you to be honest with me."

His straightforwardness was so unexpected, Kira didn't know how to respond. Her mouth opened and closed with no sound.

"Sorry," Kade said. "I should be more specific. Ella said

you had something you needed to tell me and that we shouldn't leave for Grizzly Ridge until you did. So you tell me, what's up?"

Panic raced through her. She couldn't tell him. She couldn't be honest. It would ruin everything.

Not saying anything will ruin everything.

She shook her head, the internal battle warring.

"Kira. Talk. We're not going anywhere until you tell me what's going on."

She took a deep breath, closed her eyes and before she could talk herself out of it again, the truth spilled out. "Nash is my mate."

Kira didn't open her eyes. She kept them shut so she wouldn't have to see the anger on her brother's face. Or worse, see him walking away from her again. When he didn't respond, she kept talking. "But I won't let it ruin my family. I missed you all so much and more than anything I want to go home and see—"

The pain in her gut took her words away and she doubled over, clutching her stomach. *Damn her body for reacting so violently to her emotional distress.*

When she'd recovered from the latest attack, Kira opened her eyes and was surprised to see Kade still standing there. He watched her closely. "He's your mate?"

She nodded.

"He's a wolf."

She nodded again.

She'd expected Kade to explode. To rage and yell. Or just walk away. She did not expect and was not prepared for him to be standing in front of her, calmly making statements.

"And you're going to leave."

She nodded.

"Without him."

Kira went to nod again, but finally found her voice. "Yes."

"I see."

"You do?"

Kade nodded and ran a hand through his hair. "Of course I do." He was quiet for a moment and then smiled. "So we'll leave in the morning then? Ella wants to see Old Faithful, so I'm going to take her out there this afternoon, but we'll be back later."

That was it? Just like that? Kira's mouth opened and closed again, the ability to speak evading her once again.

"Sound good?" Kade asked.

She nodded because she couldn't bring herself to do anything else.

"Great." Kade gave her a quick kiss on the cheek and turned to leave. "I'll see you later." He took two steps toward the door and stopped. Kira was sure he would turn around and say something about Nash being her mate and what that meant to her family. He was going to yell and get mad. Or maybe Ella was right and he'd be understanding after all? Maybe he'd tell her it was okay and she didn't have to choose.

Kade turned around. "One more thing," he said. "I overheard some campers talking about some dead fish down by the river. I thought you might want to know."

Kira resisted the urge to scream but she couldn't be sure what she wanted to scream about: the fact that her brother reacted so strangely or at the news he'd just delivered. Either way, she waited until Kade left, stuck the sign in the window and headed out for the river. Even if it was the last thing she did as campground manager, it would be something. And it would definitely take her mind off the mess she'd made of her life.

"Brother."

"Nolan." Nash nodded curtly. "Julia told me I could find you here." He'd driven up a back road to the shop that was kept back from the guest buildings, where they did basic tool repairs, chopped wood, and for generations, the men would hang out when they needed a break from the demands of normal life. "You hiding?"

"Wouldn't you be?"

Nash pulled up a stool next to where Nolan was tinkering with an engine of some sort. "You're certainly not selling me on the idea of this life."

Nolan scoffed. "Like you needed me to try to convince you either way. I'm not so confident to think I have any sway with you at this point."

"What's so bad that you have to hide up here, Nolan? You have a gorgeous wife and you live in the most beautiful place on earth. What's so—"

Nolan threw the screwdriver down on the bench, where it landed with a clatter. "You don't know a goddamned thing." He spun around and confronted Nash with a growl. "You think you can run off and sow your wild oats or whatever the fuck it is you wanted to do, while I'm here trying to keep all of this together. And I can't keep it together, Nash. Did you know that? It's all going to go to hell, because there are no pups. Not a fucking one."

"I knew you guys were having trouble," Nash began. "But surely others are—"

"Not one, Nash." Nolan was only barely controlling his temper. "The last pup born to our pack is ten years old."

"No. That can't be."

"It is. And do you know what that means?"

Of course he knew what it meant. If there were no pups, the pack wouldn't thrive and the reintroduction experiment would fail. To the general population, that meant there would be no pups for tourists to photograph and fawn over. For the Norths, it meant tourism would slow in their corner of the park and not only would their bloodline die out, but their contract to live and work in Yellowstone Park, on their ancestors' land, would be gone.

"But you've ensured that everyone choses suitable mates for—"

"It's not working." Nolan shook his head. "It's not just Julia and me. It's everyone. Every single mate I've arranged is the same. No pups. Nothing. We've even gone to see a specialist but it's the same story with everyone. There's nothing wrong. They can't find any reason for not conceiving. That's why you need to stop this craziness, Nash."

Of course the conversation would circle around to Nash and his betrayal of the pack. Not that he'd expected anything less when he'd made the choice to return home for the visit.

"More than ever, Nash, I need you to come home and take an appropriate mate. The pack needs you. You're our last hope at this point."

He shook his head. "That's crazy. I'm already mated. I can't just—"

"To a bear!" His brother growled as he stood. Nolan was a formidable alpha. Especially when he was angry.

But Nash wouldn't be intimidated. He rose and stood nose-to-nose with his brother.

"You're mated to a fucking bear, Nash. That's not even…"

"Don't say it."

Nolan narrowed his eyes and spat it out. "It's not natural."

"You're lucky you're my brother, or I'd teach you a

lesson right here, right now."

"Don't let that stop you."

They both fronted, stepping up to each other, their growls mixing in the air, the tension growing thicker by the second. Nolan stepped back. The bravado seeped from him and his shoulders sagged.

"I don't know what to do, Nash. They all depend on me."

The switch in his brother was so sudden, Nash stepped back in shock.

"I envy you." Nolan looked up. "Have I ever told you that?"

Nash shook his head.

"You found love? You found a mate?"

"I did." He nodded. "Fated. Did you know that's a thing bears experience?"

Nolan smiled sadly. "Wolves do too. Just not any in this pack."

"What?" He'd never heard of a fated mate pairing in wolves.

"Of course." Nolan said as if it were common knowledge. "But it hasn't happened in years, so I like to keep it quiet. It's easier that way, so no one gets any ideas of what might be out there, or what it should be like."

"What?" Nash said again. "No." He ran his hands through his hair, tugging at the ends. "No," he said again. "You didn't just say that." He spun on his heel and faced his brother. "You purposely tell members of our pack that there is no such thing as a fated mate?"

Nash couldn't believe his brother would do such a thing. *How could he knowingly and willingly keep his loved ones from such a thing as a fated mate?* Now that he'd experienced it himself firsthand, there was no way he'd go back.

The knowledge hit him like a brick.

There was no way he'd go back.

How could he ever love or pretend to love another—wolf or not—now that he knew what it was like to have a fated mate? There was no other. There was no other option for him. No way he could live any other way.

It wasn't dramatic.

It was real.

"No," he said to Nolan. "No." He shook his head and he said it again. "No, Nolan. No. You can't do that. You can't keep this from people. It's a thing. It's a very real thing that lifts your heart in a way I can't even begin to explain to you."

Nash was aware he sounded ridiculous. Especially to his brother, who'd never felt such a thing and could never be expected to understand what he was feeling. But he didn't care. He couldn't.

Passion and determination fueled him, and he stood taller. "Nolan, I feel sorry for you."

"Pardon?"

Looking at his brother, who was so concerned about reproducing and furthering his pack and failing miserably, an idea flashed through Nash's mind. "Has it ever occurred to you that part of the problem is that you have a pack full of unhappy people?"

Nolan shook his head and focused on his brother. "What? What the hell do you mean, unhappy people?"

Suddenly, it was all so clear. "Your entire pack, Nolan. They're miserable. That's why there's no pups."

Nolan shook his head and turned away. "That's ridiculous."

"Is it?"

"Of course it is. It's physiology, Nash. Boy meets girl. Boy has sex with girl. Girl has pup. It's science."

"But what if it's not?" Nash stared at his brother. "What

if it's more than that? What if that's the entire problem?"

"It's not."

Nolan refused to see what was so clear to Nash. It was about being fated. *Everything* was about being fated.

It was about Kira.

It would always be about Kira.

She was so cold.

CHAPTER THIRTEEN

The last thing Kira needed to deal with was this stupid problem of dead fish on the riverbank. But at the same time, it was a good distraction and she definitely needed a distraction because when Nash returned...well, she didn't want to think about what she would have to say when Nash returned. She was no closer to a decision either way because there couldn't possibly be a decision. There was no way she could choose.

But she couldn't think about that right now. Someone was sabotaging the campground and she was going to find out who it was. She steered the ATV past the campers, to where she knew the fish would be. Next to site 25. She'd been keeping the site free from campers just in case, but when she got there, there were no signs of rotting fish. But there was sign of Conner.

What was he doing here?

Conner was supposed to be with Sasha, checking the vacant campsites. Kira scanned the trees and spotted Sasha's dark curls just past a stand of pines. *Sasha?* Something was definitely not right.

Kira pulled up alongside Conner's ATV and cut the engine. They hadn't seen her yet, so she stayed on her ATV and watched for a minute. Conner had a shovel over his shoulder, and when Sasha got closer, Kira could make out a bucket in her hand. Whatever they were doing, Kira couldn't imagine any scenario that had to do with campsite maintenance. Her instincts fired as she left her ATV and walked toward them.

"Conner? Sasha?"

The man froze at the sound of her voice. Sasha turned and smiled. "Hey, Kira. What are you doing here? I thought you were in the office for the day? You don't need to be out here—we have this under control."

Kira tilted her head and assessed her friend, who was acting much stranger than usual. "What are you guys doing?"

It was then that Conner turned around. His mouth was pressed into a thin line, his eyes narrowed into their usual glare. She didn't care what Sasha said about the man; he was weird and grouchy. There was just something that wasn't right about him and she'd be happy when she didn't have to deal with him anymore.

"We're doing site maintenance, boss." He sneered. "Just like you told us to."

Sasha stepped forward. She glanced at Conner and her smile faded before she perked up again. "Kira, I know we said we were going to do the campsite grooming, but we got done early and we thought we should—"

"Stop." Conner held up a hand to silence her. "Can you take the bucket back to the—"

"Conner," Sasha interrupted. "I really think we should tell her—"

"Shut up. We're not telling her anything," he snarled at Sasha.

Kira's bear roared to the surface. It took all her self-control to keep her bear under wraps.

"What do you need to tell me?" She already knew the answer to the question. She'd had her suspicions early on that Conner was behind the mysterious dead fish, and in the last few minutes, everything else had fallen into place.

"Kira, it's not what it seems." Sasha stepped forward, but Conner quickly blocked her with his arm. She shot him a dirty look, but Kira didn't take her eyes off the man. She didn't trust him—she never had—and now her instincts were firing out of control.

"Oh, I'm sure everything is exactly how it looks." Conner took a few steps to Kira and while her initial instincts were to step up to him and confront him, she knew that would only bring out her bear. She couldn't risk losing control and she definitely couldn't risk shifting. Not in front of them. She had to hold it together. Kira held her ground.

"It looks to me like you're trying to hide something, Conner." She tried to keep her voice low and neutral. "And you don't need to do that. There's a chance for honesty here. Nobody needs to get in trouble."

"See, Conner?" Sasha ran to his side. If Kira hadn't been so focused on how Conner was going to react, she might have commented on how it was that her friend knew anything about the dead fish, or what exactly it was that she did know. As it was, Kira stayed focused on Conner because whatever it was, her instincts told her it wasn't going to be good.

Her instincts were dead-on. Without taking his eyes off Kira, Conner's hand shot out. "I told you to shut up." His punch connected and Sasha crumbled to the ground.

Kira glanced down. Her friend was unconscious but she couldn't go to her. Not with Conner looming. Kira's attention went back to the man, who had started to approach. His eyes were narrowed, his mouth set in a tight grimace.

"Conner." She held her hands up in what she hoped he'd feel was a non-threatening move. "I'm not sure what's happening here, but it doesn't have to get violent. No one needs to get hurt."

He continued walking.

"Are you listening to me? Conner? You're just picking up some fish you found, right? That's all that's going on here."

Confusion lined his face and it took him a moment or two to figure out that she was giving him an out. Or trying to, anyway. As soon as it registered, a grin crawled across his face and he laughed.

"You might be a bitch." He spat the words. "But you're not a stupid bitch."

So, he wasn't going to take the out.

"What are you doing, Conner? It doesn't have to be a big thing."

But it did, and they both knew it. If Conner didn't take the out she was giving him, it would definitely be a big deal. A very big deal. She'd have to report it. If he had been doing what she suspected him of—planting the fish, trapping and killing them for the purpose—it might even be considered criminal. It couldn't be ignored.

He sneered. "Like I said, you're not a dumb bitch. You took my job. The manager position was supposed to be mine."

Of course it was because of the job. She should have seen it earlier. Conner had been an asshole when they were equals, but he was downright insufferable this season. Of course it was because she'd gotten the job he'd wanted.

"It wasn't—"

"It was!" He dropped the bucket he'd been holding and his right hand disappeared behind his back. "And you just wouldn't go away." He whipped a handgun from the band of his jeans and waved it at her. Kira's heart jumped and her bear clawed to be free. But she still couldn't shift. She had to stay calm. He was still talking. More like ranting, maybe. "I gotta give you that. You just wouldn't give up. And you got the mess cleaned up so fast I couldn't even get the guests to complain enough to get you fired. And just when I was ready to kick up my efforts, she…" He pointed the gun at Sasha. "Convinced me not to. And I was stupid enough to fall for it for a little bit." He shook his head. "But when the charms of a woman wear off, the problem is still there. But now you're leaving."

"Word travels fast."

The gun swung around and pointed at her. "And I was going to make sure you never came back. That's what today was all about. But once again, you had to go and stick your nose in it and now everything is all fucked up."

There weren't a lot of options left, and Kira didn't want to know what Conner was capable of if he was backed into a corner. "You don't have to get in trouble for this." She tried to reason with him one more time. "I can just turn around and walk away. No one has to know." Her voice shook a little and she hoped like hell Conner hadn't noticed. But with a gun in his hand, she could no longer pretend that everything would be okay. Her heart raced, her breath caught in her throat, and more than anything, she wanted her bear to put an end to the situation. In her human form, she was scared, and she hated it.

Especially when he pointed the gun directly at her and said, "You know as well as I do, there isn't another way out."

Nash couldn't get out of there fast enough. Away from his brother, his backward views and everything that wasn't...Kira. Talking to Nolan, it had become clearer than ever that being fated was everything. It was his entire future. He belonged with Kira, and she with him, and yes, she may have let him walk away but it wasn't as simple as that for her. It wasn't because she didn't feel exactly the same way. Because there was no doubt in his mind that she did.

She always had.

Without Kira in his future, they didn't have one. Nash tried to explain that to Nolan. That was the reason there'd been no pups. There was no love. In his attempt to save the pack from extinction, he'd steered them the wrong way.

Not that he'd see it. He wouldn't. And he might never see it. But that didn't mean that Nash had to go down with him. When it became clear that Nolan wasn't going to listen to him, he made his apologies, because he truly was sorry to make the choice to say good-bye to his brother and to see the pain and the sense of desperation when Nolan finally realized Nash's choice. But sorry or not, he couldn't stay. Not when every bone in his body ached to be back with Kira.

Now, he raced down the highway, the need to see her increasing in urgency with every mile. At first he thought it was just because he was so anxious to see her and convince her that no matter what happened, they'd get through it together. But as the miles went by, something changed. It was different.

There was something in the air.

And then he could feel it.

Kira.

She was in trouble. Something was very wrong. He'd never been able to sense her that way before. Usually it was only when they were in animal form. Then their connection was complete. Or if one of them was shifted, there was a sense of the other. But that was different. Very different. He pressed harder on his gas pedal, urging the old truck to go faster.

Nash was familiar with the route, and fortunately, he'd chosen the less traveled highways, and traffic was light. He made good time and it wasn't long before he turned in to the campground and parked behind the office. The ATVs were gone, and the sign was in the window. It was quiet. Way too quiet. Nash ran to the cabin. It too was empty but his instincts were going crazy.

There was only one thing he could do. He dashed into the woods behind the cabin, pulling his shirt off as he went. It was risky to shift so close to people. But he didn't have another choice. Kira was in trouble and there was only one way to help her.

The second he was under cover, he closed his eyes, and let the power rip through him. His wolf was strong and—especially when his mate was concerned—fierce. The moment his paws hit the ground, he stuck his muzzle in the air and inhaled.

Kira.

Without hesitation, he took off, running through the trees and following her scent.

It would be chaos if a wolf was spotted this close to the campground, but he couldn't think of that right now. His thoughts were completely occupied by the overwhelming sense of fear emanating from his mate. She was scared and that was unacceptable.

Nash reached the river, and his ears pricked to the sound of Kira's voice.

"You don't have to do this, Conner."

Conner?

Nash bared his teeth and snarled as he stalked through the trees, until the weaselly asshole came into view. Conner's back was turned to him, but he could see Sasha in a crumpled heap next to him. But it was the look on Kira's face that made Nash's blood run cold. She was scared.

"You have no idea what I have to do." Conner's arms waved in the air, and that's when he saw it. The gun.

What the hell was Conner doing with a gun?

"This is all a big misunderstanding, Conner." Kira was trying to stay calm and be reasonable, but it was clear that Conner wasn't having any of it. "It's just a few dead fish. It's not a big deal. It doesn't have to—"

"Shut up!" Conner wiped his brow with the back of his hand. "You know as well as I do that it's not that simple."

"It doesn't have to be hard," Kira tried to reason. "I won't say anything and you can—"

"What? I can do what? Go back to work tomorrow morning?" He threw his head up and the sound that came out was a manic cackle that made Nash's blood run cold. The man had totally lost it. As quickly as the laugh started, it died. He returned his focus on Kira. "It wasn't supposed to happen like this. You were supposed to get overwhelmed with the problems of running a campground and the head office was supposed to replace you. I was *supposed* to have the job. You ruined it all. It's all your fault." Slowly and with exacting focus, Conner raised the gun and pointed it directly at Kira's head.

Nash didn't think. He only reacted. A growl ripped from his throat and he lunged out of the trees and toward Conner, who only had a fraction of a second to see the giant wolf coming at him before Nash's jaw closed down on the man's arm. A scream tore through the air as Nash landed with a thud on the man. He pinned him with his paws and stared down at his scared little face. The fear in Conner's eyes only fueled Nash's anger. He snarled and Conner squirmed helplessly beneath him.

"No!" He vaguely felt Kira's touch through his fur, but his focus remained on the man under him. "Don't." Kira's arms wrapped around him, through his fur, and he could see Conner's eyes grow wide with confusion.

Kira whispered in his ear, close enough so Conner wouldn't be able to hear. "Nash, please. Don't hurt him."

What? Of course he was going to hurt him. He'd threatened his mate. The man should die.

The man would *die.*

"No, Nash. Please." Something in her voice pierced his angry haze. Nash turned his heavy head to her, desperate to connect with her. It was the distraction Conner needed. He jerked his arm back and wiggled out from under Nash. In the flailing, Kira fell back and away. Nash growled and lunged after the man who turned, aimed the gun and—the sound was deafening. Hot-white pain ripped through him. Somewhere beside him, he heard Kira scream.

Nash's eyes clouded with pain but he couldn't let Conner win and leave his mate unprotected. With a final burst of energy, Nash growled and leapt forward, knocking Conner to the ground again. His head bounced off the ground, knocking him unconscious, but still Nash pinned the man down with one solid paw on his back while Kira ran to fetch the gun Conner dropped. The last thing he remembered before he blacked out was his sexy, strong mate looking down at him with love in her eyes. Whatever else happened, he'd know she was his. Forever.

CHAPTER FOURTEEN

Kira hadn't moved from Nash's bedside. He'd been out for over an hour, which was merciful because dealing with a gunshot wound was never easy. Shifters healed quickly, but just like humans, the bigger the injury, the longer the recovery process. And he'd been hurt badly.

Thankfully, Kade and Ella had arrived on the scene shortly after Nash lost consciousness. They'd been taking a back route on the way to the geysers, through the forest in their bear forms, when Conner had attacked. Apparently Kira sent out strong signals when she was distressed. In this case, it had worked out well, because there was no way she would have been able to take care of the situation on her own.

Together they'd loaded Nash—who'd already shifted back into his human form—onto an ATV and raced him back to the cabin, where Kira extracted the bullet. She didn't have a lot of experience with injuries like Nash's, but growing up with three brothers and a culture where you couldn't just go to the local doctor for treatment, she wasn't a complete stranger to blood and major injuries. She did her best and prayed for no infection so his shifter blood could deal with the healing.

She had his hand in hers, her head heavy from exhaustion when she heard the creak of the bedroom door behind her.

"Kira? Can I come in?"

She nodded in response to her brother's question. She would have liked to avoid him and everything else beyond the walls of the room where she sat, but she couldn't ignore everything that had gone down and she was incredibly thankful Kade had been there to help her out.

"How is he?" Kade pulled up a chair next to her and sat.

She shrugged. "He hasn't opened his eyes yet." A tear slipped down her cheek. It was the first one she'd let herself cry.

Kade put his hand on her shoulder and squeezed. "He'll be okay."

She nodded, but didn't look at her brother. She needed to change the subject if she had any chance at holding herself together. "Is everything...did you...what happened?"

"Don't worry. It's all good. We took care of it."

Kira wiped her eyes and looked at her brother, who had a shit-eating grin on his face. "What does that mean?"

"It means that Conner won't bother you anymore." His grin grew wider. "Your friend Sasha woke up and she was pissed." He chuckled a little. "Apparently she knew all kinds of things about our buddy Conner. Like, not only was he responsible for the rotten fish and trying to get you fired, but it wasn't his first time doing something like this."

"What?"

"Yup. Turns out he has a long history of petty grievances, but this situation got a little out of hand. Of course he tried to pull out, but he was in too deep. According to Sasha, he's not the most stable tree in the forest either."

Kira tried not to laugh at her brother's assessment. "What does that mean?"

"Bit of a history of mental illness as well." Kade shook his head. "I don't know what your friend saw in him, but the info was certainly helpful. And there's nothing like a pissed-off woman to give you all the details," he said.

Nash's hand twitched in hers, and Kira's eyes shot back to her mate. Her eyes scanned him for a few moments but there were no more signs that he was waking. She turned back to Kade. "So what happened?"

"I recorded his confession." He held up his phone. "And then I threatened him with basically ruining his life if he didn't immediately get out of Yellowstone and never come back."

"But he didn't come back to the house to grab his things or anything."

Kade shook his head. "Nope. I gave him a ten-minute head start but told him if he wasn't miles away, I'd drag his ass into the police station myself. I think he got the point." He grinned again, and actually looked as though he'd enjoyed himself, which he probably did.

"Thank you." Kira's shoulders slumped again. "I don't know what I would have done if—"

"Forget it. That's what I'm here for. To protect you. You're my sister—it's what I do."

They were silent for a few minutes, Kade's hand still squeezing hers. Her other hand held tight to Nash. Her two worlds, one in each hand. But it was no longer a choice she was willing to make.

"Kade, I—"

"I think we—"

They spoke at the same time. One look at her brother and she knew he knew her choice. After everything that had happened, how could he not?

"I need to tell you something," she started. "I told you before that Nash is my...he's my mate." Kade nodded. "But he's more than that. I don't know how it happened," she continued, needing to fill the silence. "He's a wolf and I'm a bear, and...it's all so crazy, but from the moment I met him, there was something there between us and when we..."

"I know what you're going to say, Kira."

"Shifted, it was just like being with him was the most natural thing in the world," she continued, not hearing Kade. "It's indescribable. It's like I was—what? What did you say?"

Kade smiled. "I said, that I know what you're going to say. I've known from the moment I met him and saw you together." He shrugged.

Kira's head spun. *He knew*. He knew that she was going to choose Nash over her family and he wasn't upset. He wasn't yelling at her, demanding that this time she choose her family over her mate. She shook her head. "But he's a wolf."

Kade chuckled. "I can see that."

"But I'm a bear."

He laughed again and shook his head. "Kira." He squeezed her hand. "I know that too. But he's your mate." She nodded, although it wasn't a question. "And you're fated."

Her head shot up. *How did he know that?*

"I can see it all over you, sister. I just wasn't sure you knew it. Look, I'm not going to lie and tell you that I'm excited that your mate is a dog." He winked, but otherwise his face was a mask of seriousness. "But fated is fated. And if you tell me that's it, I believe you."

"I told you that once before." The reminder stung, and

Kade flinched as well.

"That was a mistake," he said softly. "We both know better now."

Tears filled her eyes. "So you're not making me choose?"

"God no, Kira." Kade looked genuinely shocked. "I'm the first to admit that I may not have always been understanding when it came to love and mates. But Ella changed that for me, and now I know what it's really like. Because of that, I know without a doubt that you can't choose. It would physically destroy you if I made you pick between your mate and your family. It's not something I'd ever do. I love you, sis. We all do. And that means we'll love Nash, too. Besides, he took a bullet for you. If that's not the sign of a good man, I don't know what is. Dog or not." He smiled and wrapped his arm around her.

"But yesterday..." She was confused. *So* confused. It was only the day before that her brother had stood silently, judging her because her mate was a wolf, and now he was happily telling her that it would all be okay? It didn't make sense.

"What about yesterday?"

"I told you about Nash, and you..."

"Didn't say anything?"

She nodded.

"What would you have had me say, Kira? You told me Nash was your mate. And then you proceeded to tell me that you were going to leave without him."

The realization hit her as Kade explained it.

"I knew if you were fated, *really* fated," he said pointedly, "it wouldn't be a choice at all. The fact that you were willing to leave without him told me everything I needed to know."

Shame filled her and she looked down at her feet. She

should have known. She should have trusted her heart. Trusted her brother. *Dammit, she should have trusted herself.* "I'm sorry," she whispered. "None of this would have happened if I hadn't have—"

"It doesn't matter." Kade put a hand on her shoulder to still her. "What's done is done."

But it wasn't done. Because of her, Kira's brothers had been cast out. Their whole lives had changed. "It's all my fault, Kade. Don't you see that? I didn't know my heart the first time. With Ryan. And everything that happened, it's all my—"

"We have you to thank."

"Thank?"

Kade chuckled. "I agree, it wasn't the easiest way to go about a life change, but because of you, Kira, we were all able to find our mates and live the lives we want to. Because you were brave enough to go after what you wanted, smart choice or not, everything is working out the way it's supposed to."

She let that sink in. Everything that had happened to them. The Ridge, their mates, and even Axel's new cub: it was because of the choice she made.

"Look." Kade shook her gently and forced her to look up at him. "There is no point beating yourself up over this. It's done. The important thing now is we have you back and you have your mate. Your true *fated* mate." He nodded his head toward Nash. "Everything else we can work through."

A flood of different emotions washed through her. There was still so much she wanted to say, but finally it came down to one thing. "Thank you," she said simply.

"For what?"

"For being my brother. For having my back and for coming to find me. I'm happy to have you back."

He wrapped her up in a tight bear hug. "Little sister, you have no idea how much we missed you." He released her and flashed her a mischievous smile. "Also, did you not know that Axel's mate, Harper, is only half bear? I mean, we love her, and she's a hybrid. I'm sure we can handle a dog hanging around, too." She smacked him and he laughed.

She hadn't known that about Harper. There was so much she didn't know. But she would.

But first, she had to make Nash understand how much she loved and needed him.

She just hoped it wasn't too late.

The pain in his abdomen flared with every breath he took and Nash wished again for unconsciousness. That way he wouldn't have to deal with the red-hot pain. Damn, he'd never been shot before, a fact he was intensely thankful for because fuck, it hurt. Kira's voice filtered through his fog, and all traces of his pain washed away.

He'd do it again.

And again.

He'd take a bullet for that woman a hundred times over if he needed to. She was everything.

Sleep called to him, but he fought through the exhaustion and forced his eyes open. Instead of his eyes landing on the vision of his love, they fluttered open to...her brother.

"Good morning, dog." Kade grinned down at him and then he was shoved out of the way and his face was replaced by Kira. She stood over him, concern and love in her eyes.

"Hey." She stroked his cheek and he closed his eyes to absorb the pleasure of the touch. "How are you feeling?"

"I...I..."

"Don't try to talk." Kira's hands fluttered over him and finally landed on his face. She pressed her lips to his in a kiss that was both unexpected and absolutely perfect.

"Give the man a chance to heal, jeez."

But her kiss was healing in all the right ways. Nash lifted an arm and threaded his fingers through her hair, holding her in place. The taste of her on his lips was exactly what he needed, because it meant... *What did it mean?*

She pulled away and tears filled her eyes. *Was that a good-bye?* He would absolutely not accept a good-bye. She was his. They were fated. And that meant *everything.*

"What's wrong?" He found his voice. "Are you hurt? He didn't hurt you, did he?"

She shook her head, but still didn't speak.

"I'll leave you two alone," Kade said.

Nash had already forgotten he was in the room. He only had eyes for his mate. There was a soft click of the door and then they were alone.

"Are you okay?"

She nodded.

"He didn't hurt you?"

"No."

"Kira, I—"

"Nash, we—"

He managed a small smile. "Let me go first. Please."

She nodded.

"Kira. When I sensed that you were in trouble earlier, it scared the hell out of me. And when I saw him...that asshole, pointing a gun at you...well, I can't even..." She grabbed his hand and squeezed. "It terrified me that I could lose you and I knew in that moment, I would never be able to survive without you. I won't survive without you. But I already knew that."

"Nash, I—

"I can't, Kira. We're fated. You know it and I know it. We were meant to be together, and your family and my family, well...they'll just have to—"

"Be okay with it."

He shook his head, not sure he heard her properly. "What?"

Her smile gave him a thrill. "They'll be okay with it," she repeated. "They *are* okay with it. But even if they weren't...Nash, it's you. It's always you. It will always be you." Tears streamed down her face, but she was still smiling. "I was so worried," she said. "I thought I lost you. And you're right. I can't survive without you. And I won't."

Bullet wound or not, he didn't care. The pain was white-hot as he pulled himself into a sitting position, but it didn't matter.

"Nash, you're going to open your wound," she protested but didn't try to stop him.

He was healing fast. Besides, it wouldn't matter if his body healed if his heart wasn't pieced back together.

"Kira Jackson, I need you more than I need the air in my lungs. I thought I could step back and let you have time to figure out what you needed to do with your family, but I can't."

"Nash, I—"

"No. I can't." He shook his head. "I just can't sit back and wait for you to make a choice that could destroy us both. I know the pull of family is strong. I know. I...I feel it too. But I also know something else." He threaded his fingers through hers and pressed them to his lips. "Nolan and the pack, they aren't my future. They aren't my family. You are. It will always be you. I need you to tell me you feel the same."

"I do."

Her voice was so soft, he wasn't sure he heard her properly.

"What?"

"I do," she said again. "I feel exactly the same, Nash. That's what I'm trying to tell you. From the moment I let you walk away, I was empty. I can't live without you either. And I won't."

"Come here." She did as he asked and sat on the side of his bed. He tugged her toward him, needing to feel her.

"Nash, I'll hurt you."

"No, babe." He pulled her into him with as much strength as he could manage. "You'll never hurt me." His hands cupped her cheeks and as he held her face in his hands, he held his whole world.

He kissed her softly. There'd be time for heat later when he was completely healed. Although with each passing moment he could feel his strength returning. His cock twitched under the bed covers, obviously feeling more than healed. But no. He had a lifetime to show her exactly how he felt about her. For now, having his mate in his arms was all he needed. Nash nestled into Kira's neck and breathed deep, inhaling the sexy scent that was all her. He let it fill him, but there was something different. He stopped, and then leaned in and took another breath.

"What's wrong?" Next to him, Kira shifted so she could look into his eyes. "Nash?"

"Nothing," he answered honestly. "I think my senses are just a little off right now."

She sat up and smoothed his hair back off his face. "Of course they are. You're healing. Let your body work."

He smiled what he hoped was a reassuring smile, but his mind was still working. "Tell me about Grizzly Ridge," he said. "When do we leave?"

"You want to go visit?"

"Of course, babe. More than anything I want to meet your family and see where you're from."

She nodded enthusiastically, happiness and excitement all over her face. "We can leave as soon as you're feeling up to it. I put in for holiday time, but…"

"But you'd like to stay at Grizzly Ridge?" Nash already knew Kira wouldn't want to return to Yellowstone once she got home. The pull of family was strong. Especially if they accepted him as her mate.

"I don't know for sure, but…"

"It's okay, babe. We'll figure it out. Together."

She dropped a kiss on his nose before she sat up again. "I want to hold my new little niece in my arms and rock her and sing to her and never let her go. I've always wanted to be a—" She cut herself off. They hadn't talked about what their future would look like. Nash hadn't even really thought about it, considering they were different species, but… "I guess we still have a lot to talk about, don't we."

Something clicked in Nash's head and all the pieces fit together.

A slow grin spread across his face as he realized what the shift in her scent meant.

"Nash?" Worry filled her voice. "You do want cubs…or…well, kids one day. Don't you?"

Nash took Kira's hands in his own and pulled her down one more time so he could be sure. "Babe," he whispered in her ear. "I think we should leave for Grizzly Ridge right away so we can meet our baby's cousin."

"What?" She jerked up. "Our baby?"

He nodded and her hands went immediately to her stomach.

"But how…you…how did you…I didn't even know."

"Canine senses," he said, as if it explained everything. "It doesn't matter, babe." Tears pooled in her eyes, but he knew this time they were happy tears. "All that matters is that I love you, Kira." Nash slid his hand over hers and rested it over her stomach. "And we're going to be a family."

CHAPTER FIFTEEN

Four weeks later...

Kira didn't think she would ever tire of holding little Lily in her arms. Her new little niece was the most precious thing she'd ever seen and she'd fallen in love at first sight. In fact, Kira had fallen in love at first sight with everything and everyone in Grizzly Ridge.

Her brothers had greeted her home with open arms. Not that Grizzly Ridge was the home she remembered, but from the moment she'd set foot on the mountain, Kira knew she was truly home. Luke's mate Chloe and Axel's mate Harper had accepted her like a sister and even Nash had experienced a warmer welcome than anyone had expected.

There was some initial suspicion, especially from Luke. But Kade explained to everyone what Nash had done for Kira, earning him a great deal of respect from the men, but it was seeing Kira and Nash together that won everyone over.

The love they had for each other just grew with every day.

Just like the baby in her belly.

She still hadn't told anyone they were expecting. Mostly because she and Nash had decided that with the excitement of returning to Montana and getting settled into the Ridge, it was best if they kept it to themselves. Also, there were so many unknowns. Would the baby be a cub? Or a pup? They'd decided to keep their little secret under wraps, at least until they figured out a few of the details. Or until she couldn't hide it anymore. Kira's stomach was expanding much quicker than she would have expected. If she did the calculations, she was barely three months along. She shouldn't be starting to show already. But then again, there was a lot she didn't know about pregnancy. Let alone a shifter pregnancy.

Not that it mattered yet, anyway. Kira had her hands full with little Lily. She'd fallen easily into the role of auntie, and Harper was more than happy to have the help. Especially considering the business of the ranch had only increased due to the summer season, and besides taking care of most of the day-to-day operations, Axel had surprised Kira and Nash with the construction of their very own cabin. Nash had been right: now that they were on Grizzly Ridge, Kira was not in a hurry to leave.

"I'm so sorry." Harper appeared in the great living room from the kitchen. "Are you okay with her for another minute? I just want your opinion on something."

"Of course." Kira rocked the sleeping bundle. "I'm in no hurry. What do you need opinions on?"

"Hold on." Harper turned and called toward the kitchen, "Ella. Come in here."

The swinging door opened and Ella came in carrying a tray full of cupcakes, with Chloe right behind her. "It's wedding cake tasting time."

"Wedding cakes? Yum."

"Right?" Harper sat next to her on the couch and gave

her baby girl a gentle kiss before she smiled up at Kira. "I'm so glad you're here, Kira. It's like things weren't complete without you and now that you're back..." Tears welled in her eyes. "Well, I'm just so glad you're here and we're all together."

"And you can finally get married." Ella laughed as she set the tray down. "But you're going to need to get those emotions in check if you're going to make it through the ceremony."

Harper accepted the tissue Chloe held out to her and wiped her eyes. "I can't help it. I'm just so happy." She broke into another sob and Kira and Chloe exchanged glances.

"You'll see." Harper pointed her finger at Ella. "If you're not all hormonal yet, you will be."

Ella rubbed her belly, which was definitely popping out in a cute round bump, and smiled. As soon as they'd arrived home from Yellowstone, she'd told the rest of the family that they were expecting their own cub in a few months. Kira couldn't help but be secretly pleased she'd known first. It helped her feel even a little bit more connected with everything she'd missed while she'd been gone.

"Okay, okay," Chloe said, drawing their attention back to the cakes. "Let's start tasting. I didn't think I'd be so into this wedding thing, but it's super fun."

"I told you!" Harper clapped her hands together. "I don't know why all shifters don't get married. You're missing out on so much." Harper took the baby gently from Kira's arms. "Let me go lay her down so we can eat cake."

She was sorry to see the gentle weight of the baby go, but more than happy to indulge in some cake. Kira had been absolutely ravenous since arriving back at the Ridge.

Ella reached for a cupcake and passed it to Kira.

"Maybe you're on to something, *muy hermana.*"

"What do you mean?" Harper sat down next to Ella. "Weddings?"

"*Sí.*"

"She's right," Chloe said. "Weddings are a human thing, but maybe that's only because we never thought they *could* be a shifter thing?"

Kira nodded. The idea of having a wedding wasn't totally unappealing. In fact, the more she helped Harper with the details of hers, the more she could imagine herself doing it, too. Which was crazy, because weddings *were* a human thing. The only reason Axel had agreed to it was because it was important to Harper, who had only recently discovered her shifter side.

"It could be a business, Harper," Kira piped up. "Organizing shifter weddings. It could be the next big thing. A service people didn't even know they needed."

"As if we don't have enough to do." Chloe chose a cake of her own. "But I do like the idea," she admitted.

"Well, maybe we're too busy to do it." Harper tapped a finger on her lips. "But I know the perfect person for such a thing."

"Bree."

"Bree."

Chloe and Kira said at once. The name popped into Kira's head immediately. She'd been a long-time resident of Boulder Creek, the town next to the one she'd grown up in. She wasn't a shifter herself, but she was one of the few humans who knew all about them. And she definitely had a sense of style. She ran a store, Bree's Knees, that catered to the curvy girls that shifters often were, or preferred to mate with.

"She's perfect," Harper agreed. "I'll call her in the

morning and tell her our brilliant idea."

The women spent the rest of the morning giggling over cake choices, talking about Harper's wedding and Ella's pregnancy. It was perfect, and Kira had never felt happier. Except for her time with Nash. But at the Ridge, she had it all, and when lunch time drew nearer and the women all scattered to their various duties, Kira packed up a picnic basket and snuck off to meet her own lunch date in the woods.

Nash didn't waste any time getting to their meeting spot, tucked back in the woods next to the creek. Ever since they'd arrived on the Ridge, they'd been kept busy. Not that Nash minded. He liked to be busy and Kira's brothers had all been very welcoming. Except for a few tense moments with Luke, who, from what Nash could tell, was just trying to test Nash's worth as his sister's mate, things had been good. He liked the guys, and he enjoyed the physical labor.

But there was another type of physical labor he enjoyed more.

Nash's cock stiffened at the sight of his mate, who was laid out, naked, on a picnic blanket, her eyes closed, the sun warming her creamy skin. Kira's arms were tucked under her head, exposing the now silver mark of his mate bite. Her breasts, fuller now with the pregnancy, stood lush and ready for his attention.

He moved slowly and silently toward her, shedding his clothes as he went.

When he reached the blanket, he dropped to his knees and started to crawl up Kira's body with a low growl rumbling in his throat.

Her eyes opened, as if she already knew he was there.

"Hey, handsome."

"Gorgeous." He kissed his way up her leg until he reached the cleft of her legs.

"Hungry?"

"More than you know." She let out a delicious gasp as he spread her legs and used the flat of his tongue to lick her crease. "Yummy." He lifted his head to see her looking down at him, with heat in her eyes. Her hands twisted through his hair, urging him on, and Nash was happy to oblige. For the next few minutes, he licked and sucked and teased until his perfectly sexy mate was screaming her pleasure up to the trees.

When she was satisfied, Nash pulled himself up, stopping to kiss Kira's swelling belly before he pressed his mouth to hers. "Hi there, beautiful."

"Hi yourself." She giggled and, still naked, sat up to get the picnic basket she'd prepared. She handed him a sandwich. "How was your morning? How's the cabin coming?"

"About that…" She eyed him and Nash purposely looked away. He knew Kira wanted to wait before telling anyone about their pregnancy, but he was no longer convinced it was a good idea. "I think you should come by the site after lunch. I want to show you the progress."

Nash immediately regretted saying anything at all, only because Kira wasn't the type of woman to sit by and do or say nothing after a statement like that. Lunch was finished in short order and far too soon, she'd packed up, put on her clothes and was demanding to visit the site. Date over.

"You know, it could have waited." He laughed and slid his hand in hers as they made their way to the site. All of the brothers had their own cabins away from the main lodge. It was their way of having privacy from their guests who stayed in the rooms in the lodge. As a sign of acceptance, and a welcome home gift, the brothers had offered to build Nash and Kira a cabin. It was a generous offer, and Nash had been enjoying working on the project, but they'd reached a point in construction where a decision needed to be made.

The foundation had been laid, and walls were starting to go up, but Nash had stopped word on the back side of the house until he talked to Kira. There was something he needed to go over with her. "What do you think?" he asked after she had a moment to look it over.

She looked confused, as he thought she might. "Can you walk me through it?"

"Of course." Nash held tight to her hand. "This is the living room." He pointed to the front area. "There'll be a kitchenette area along the back wall. I thought we'd mostly use the main kitchen in the lodge." She nodded her agreement. "This is the bathroom." They walked over to the space marked on the floor. "And our bedroom."

"Right." Kira nodded. "But what's this? Why is there all this space here?"

She pointed to the space in the back. The space Nash was struggling with.

"This will be the baby's room." Kira looked at him, waiting for the rest of it. "I think we should make two."

"Two?" She stared at him as if he'd lost his mind. "Like, two bedrooms?"

Nash nodded.

"Why would we do that?"

He'd suspected from the very beginning that there was something a little unusual about Kira's pregnancy, but watching her since they'd arrived at the Ridge, Nash was almost sure of what was happening.

"I think we should tell the others."

"Tell the others what?"

Shit.

The brothers were back from their own lunch break. Nash had been so wrapped up in Kira, he hadn't noticed them come up.

"What do you think, Kira?" Axel gave his sister a quick hug. There was a lot of love in the Jackson family, particularly when it came to their little sister. "Do you like it?"

"I do." She smiled. "A lot. Thank you so much, guys."

"But?" Kade noticed her hesitancy right away. "What's wrong?"

Luke flashed Nash a look. *No doubt just being the overprotective brother. Again.*

"Nash was just showing me the floor plan and—"

"Right," Luke interrupted. "You have something to tell us."

"That was a private conversation." Nash shook his head. "It was between Kira and me."

"Sounded like you had something to tell us." Luke stepped forward and Kira put a hand on her brother's shoulder.

"Luke. Seriously." Kira looked to Nash. "What's going on? With the house?"

He took in a breath and let it out slowly. There was no point keeping quiet. "Okay," he started. "We're almost done closing in the main floor."

"But Nash had us stop on this room," Kade offered.

"I did." Nash walked toward the room in question. "I was just telling Kira I think we should make it into two rooms instead of one."

"Why?" It was Axel who asked. "I thought the idea of the room was for when you had a cub one day."

Nash nodded.

"You can always add another room later if you expand

your family."

Nash raised his eyebrows.

"Isn't that still the plan?"

He nodded.

"But that'll be awhile," Luke said and looked between them. "I mean, first you have to have one cub."

Nash nodded again and looked at Kira, who looked just as confused as her brothers. "Right," Nash said slowly. He watched Kira closely as he spoke. "And if that were to happen, I think *everyone* should be prepared for the possibility of twins."

"Twins?" Kade almost choked on the word, no doubt thinking of Ella.

"There *are* twins in the family, after all." Nash looked pointedly between Kira and Kade but his eyes rested on Kira, whose face had gone white.

She opened her mouth; her lips formed the word but no sound came out. *Twins.*

Nash nodded and went to her. His hands went straight to her stomach, which had swelled much faster than it should have. And then there was her scent. He was surprised the others couldn't sense it. Her hormones were so strong, it had changed her scent almost at once. He'd suspected that day that there was something different about her pregnancy, but as the days went on, the more positive he was.

"Nash?" Her voice was quiet. "Twins?"

He nodded. "I think so."

Tears flooded her eyes. Her emotions were always so close to the surface in the past weeks. "Oh my God. I can't even...I don't know....oh my God. Twins." She laughed as the tears fell down her face.

Nash didn't care that they were surrounded by her older brothers; at that moment, Kira was the only person in the world. Her and their unborn babies. He took her face in his hands and kissed her with all the love he felt for her and the lives she was carrying within her.

There were whoops of shock and surprise around them as her brothers put it all together and shouted out their celebrations. Somehow, in the next few minutes, the women arrived with bottles of champagne and sparkling apple juice. All together, outside of what was to be Kira and Nash's new family home, they toasted to love and life and family.

It wasn't the family Nash had expected, and the loss of his own still tugged at something deep inside, but that no longer mattered. Because his whole world, his entire future, was right there on Grizzly Ridge.

THE END

Elena Aitken

Hers to Take

Make sure you visit Elena Aitken on her website at:
www.elenaaitken.com

And hang out with her on her Facebook page for up-to-date information on the release of this new series.

https://www.facebook.com/elenaaitken.author

I have the best job in the world because I get to write the stories of my heart and it's my hope that you enjoy reading them as much as I love writing them. Whenever I get the chance, I escape to the mountains to soak up the inspiration and plot my next story.

To learn more about Elena Aitken and her other books, please visit www.elenaaitken.com
Twitter - @elenaaitken
Facebook - www.facebook.com/elenaaitken.author

Hers to Take

Made in the USA
Columbia, SC
04 March 2021